The Cool World

The Cool World

The Cool World

A NOVEL BY

WARREN MILLER

BOSTON · Little, Brown and Company · TORONTO

Published simultaneously in Canada
by Little, Brown & Company (Canada) Limited

PRINTED IN THE UNITED STATES OF AMERICA

To Abby

The Cool World

The first time I see Priest

They call him Priest because he always wear black. Black suits with thin tight pants. One day some body see him an they say. "Man you always in black. Like a priest. You the hep priest Man." So that how come he is call priest.

Priest say to me. "Man I tellin you. You aint gonna find anything good as this for the kind of bread I askin for. You can go up an down this street a thousan times an you aint gonna find it."

I say to Priest. "Man I dont have *time* to go up and down this street a thousan times. I in a big hurry. But shitman that aint worth no 15 dollas."

Priest he laugh. He taken the piece out of the draw again. It a short-barl 45 with that crisscross lines on the butt. Priest dont flip it around like a cowboy. He cool. He hold it in his big hand like it somethin sweet an he smile at it.

"It aint gonna smile back at you Man." I say. An Priest he laugh an not lookin smash a roach under his heel. He say. "Only 9 hundred and 99 thousan left in Harlem now Man. I killin em all. I leavin rats an mice to the City but I killin the roaches my-self."

"If that piece smile back at you Priest I would give you the 15. But that piece . . ."

"Im a big roach killer from Georgia." Priest say. He talken like I aint even in the room no more. "Thats me." He say. "That is me. Town of Spartacus."

"That piece aint been worth no fifteen dollas since you was a little boy Priest." I tell him.

He just set there smilin an heftin the weapon.

"Kill roaches with it Priest. I aint payin that kind of bread for no iron like that. Thats so old that piece thats so old I wouldnt be surprise Lincoln wasnt killed with it."

"You aint got 15." Priest say lookin at me from under his eyes an leanin back in that rounback chair that tweaks and snitters evytime he move. "I comin a far piece from Spartacus Georgia an I dont aim to go back. That is why this piece is 15 Man an that is why ifn you want it 15 is whut you are goin a pay." Then he put the piece back in the draw an close it slow an quiet. When it close it make a noise like this. Slump. He close the draw. Slump.

"Oh I got the bread Priest." I say an I touch my pocket easy showin him where it is. "Right here Man where my hand is." All a time that pocket empty an my hand touchin ony my leg. But I playin it cool.

Priest put his big hand on the draw knob. It is brass and it made like the snout of some kinda animal. A fox or somethin like that. Got green spots on it. Priest touch it with his thum an next finger.

He say. "Maybe you like to hold it in you hand you self. Get the feel of it."

"Man." I say to him. "Man I know what a piece feel like."

Priest. He laugh and sit back an that chair snitters and snatters. "I tell you whut." he say. "Duke I tell you whut. I hold it faw a day or two. Give you time to think about it. You go up and down this street a thousan time . . ."

At the door I say. "Priest I don know how you do any bizness at all."

Priest he put his hands on his belly an he laugh and the chair laugh.

"I make out." He say.

Door open. I say. "Okay Priest. Maybe I see you aroun."

"You be back." Priest say lookin at me. "I know you be back Man. I can tell you want this bad Man. Cause you need it."

An I seen that piece right through the table top. Lace cloth an all. Gleamin black in the black draw with the brass head on it. A fox or some kinda animal.

I went down the steps. Three flights. Dogs barkin behin the doors an evry door with an iron flange to keep out the jimmys. Chick in a sweater comes up the stairs. Big smile. "Hi Duke." she say. Sue Randolph her name. "Keep movin big tit." I say. An I dont even look at her. I keepin away from girls for a while. At that time.

Outside. Summer waitin for me. "You get it?" Summer want to know.

I keep walkin.

Summer say. "How much he want?"

"15"

"Shitman. Ats a lot of bread."

Water truck come by then an slick the street. All the crap pushed into the gutters garbage boxes butts bottles cundums news papers all hissin an skewin into the gutters.

"Watch it Man." Summer say.

But I aready moved. Fast. Im fast.

Summer look at me and say. "Man."

When we get to the School bilding Summer say. "Shitman we finely movin."

Three big buses lined up waitin. Mister Shapiro say. "Custis. Summer. You almost missed the outing. Line up now boys."

We go to the bus with a card stuck to the door sayin

8TH GRADE

MR SHAPIRO

an we got on. Handy savin me a seat up front. "You get it?" He say. An then the others stick they faces over the back of my seat. "You get it Duke?" They all askin.

Mr. Shapiro get on the bus. He say. "All right boys. Now I know we are going to enjoy this trip."

Who am I?

I rather think about bein Mighty Mouse and flyin through the air an like that. But now I here at this place an they askin me questions — whut I dream about & whut I think about & whut about my mother my father an like that. Man you start thinkin about things like that an it give you the sweats like a junkie.

Some times back home when I was back home in Harlem I laid there on the beat up sofa with the chitterin springs and I uset to think about who am I. But I give it up. It dont get you know where.

You start figurin out who am I an why am I an why am I here in Harlem — an Man they aint no end to it. You end up askin your self whut is the world an whut was the world before it was the world. An did GOD make this world. An who made GOD.

Where he come from? Shitman they aint no end to it an you just end up scared.

Man—you ask Why should I be *me*—how I *get* to be me—why am I me here & not somplace else—& you just end up scared like you was walkin down a empty street at night. So scared it running out you ears. Or you end up thumpin out a hymn like Gramma Custis in some fool Church.

Outside her an my mother the only relative I ever see is my Aunt May. Once or twice a year my Aunt May come over from Brooklyn where she live to see us. She a big woman not skinny like my mother an when she come up the steps she puff like an engine. She always stand at the door with her hand on her heart. She say. "When you folks gonna move to a projeck with a elevator?"

My mother say. "Soons the City let us in. If I had as many kids as you Id a been *in* a long time ago. But I only got the one child you know May."

Aunt May look at me. "An just look at him." She say. "Just you *look* at him." She take an pull me over to her and look at my face. "He one of us all right." She say smilin at me. "He a Custis sure enough."

"He whut GOD give us." Gramma say.

"Got his fathers bones." My mother say.

Aunt May tell me. "Boy I surely do hope you have

7

got you full growth. You get any taller an we wont be able to see you face no more."

"I aint so tall. Theys boys my age taller than me."

"How old you now Richard? Fourteen?"

"He was 14 las month." My mother say. "On the 8th."

"I make it out to be the 7th day." Gramma say.

"I guess I know when my own and only child was born." My mother say.

Gramma tell her. "You dint know nothin that day Girl."

"How you do in school Richard?" Aunt May ask me.

"Jabberin an cryin. Cryin an jabberin. That all you know that day." Gramma sayin.

"Its o.k. I be glad when it over an I can get a job."

"Un huh." Aunt May say.

"Man at the liquor store give me a promise. He gonna give me a job soon as I gradjuate." I tell her. She believe anything.

"That nice clean work Richard." She say. "Clerkin in the liquor stores is nice clean work."

Clerkin in the liquor stores. Oh Man. Dont she know who she talkin to. Duke Custis. War Lord of the Royal Crocadiles. I been knifed 7 times an I got 9 stitches in my head from where a sonofabitch Wolve bastard hit me with a radio aireal off a car. From be-

8

hind. Aunt May live aroun here an not way the hell over in Brooklyn she know *I have a rep!*

When I come walkin down the street the people say. "Here come Duke. He cool. He got heart."

An on a Friday night Friday night is a big night people watch me walkin down the street. They see me strut. They know a rumble on. They know we are goin down on the Wolves.

"Tonight the night Duke Man?" They ask me.

I just smile and keep movin bouncin on my heels.

"You goin down on the Wolves tonight Duke?"

"You give it to em Duke."

"Kill em Duke."

Someday I come walkin down the street they all look at me with respect an say. "There goes a cold killer. Here come Duke Custis. He a cold killer." Then evrybody pay attention—an listen when I talk— I be the top of the heap an when I push they stay push.

I keep movin. Some time I wave a hand to em. The coolies look at me. Coolies dont swing with the gang. They are out an by themselves alone. It make em mad to see me when I strut. Screw them. Aint no place for coolies in this world.

Keep walking. My rumble strut. Everybody know somethin is cookin. Here come Duke. He got a rep

9

Man. Man he got heart. I swingin with the gang tonight. They all waitin for me. Duke Custis. The War Lord of the Royal Crocadiles.

Aunt May an Gramma Custis an my mother talkin about the old days in Alabama. Shitman I just turn off when they go off on that kick.

Before she leave Aunt May she look aroun an she say to my mother. "Dolly. I dont see any indications that you have a husband anymore."

My mother say. "No May right now at this time I dont happen to have a husband."

"Fred walk out?" Aunt May ask her.

"Oh him. That Fred. I threw him out long ago."

"The Lawd frowns his eyes on a man whut gambles and drinks." Gramma say.

"Well whut husband you without now anyway?" Aunt May ask.

My mother say. "Charles Osborne his name."

"He walk out?"

"It aint so much he walk out as so much that he never come back." My mother say.

"How long he been away?" My Aunt May ask at the door.

"A week today."

"Almos 2 weeks." Gramma say. "I make it closer to 2."

"Well maybe he still come back." Aunt May sayin.

"Oh I dont have a single solitary doubt about that."
My mother say. "He be back all right."

Oh Man. I sit there laughin in side. He aint comin
back. When a Man go he go.

Why I need the piece

So we go down to Wall Street that day Mister Shapiro he took us. Shapiro is okay he aint always yellen at us like the rest of them. Some of the teachers tell you. "Stay out. Dont come to school an we wont report you. You co operate with me an I will co operate with you." They dont want to be bothered. Mister Shapiro he aint like that. A little man. He look worried all the time. Got lines in his forhead like they been cut in.

First we went to the George Washington Museum. It has this big statue of him out front. The place where we went was the cellar of this building where they got cases full of things from histry. Mister Shapiro he lead us around explainin this an that. Histry make Mister Shapiro get all hopped up you know. He say. "Think of it boys where you standen right now

maybe the Father of our Country once stood." Evrybody look down at they feet.

Handy and Summer an me was in the back an all
they talken about was the piece. Handy say. "Shitman
you get yourself a piece you gonna be President of the
Crocadiles. Aint no doubt about that."

"Where you hear that?" I ask him.

He just shrug. He just shrug. "Hear it around."
He say. "Blood is getten old. He gonna be 20 soon.
He cant swing with the gang for ever. Time he moved
up."

Summer say to me. "Whut kind of piece you say it
was Duke man?" Summer talk like a big shot because
his father a big man in the numbers.

I tell him it was a Colt.

"Birettas is better." Summer say.

Handy say. "Dint Priest spread the word whut he
had was a Biretta?"

"That whut he say. But whut he got is a Colt."
I tell them.

"I like the Biretta my self." Summer say.

"Biretta the best Duke." Handy tell me. "That is
one sweet piece the Biretta."

"I like the Biretta." Summer say.

"Biretta is for women." I tell them.

"Now hold on Man." Summer say. "Now jus a

13

minute. Lemme tell you something Man. Colt dont have the improvements Man. Why shitman them Colts is the same motheren piece they was usen at Cussers Last Stan."

Then Handy get into it. Like he knew whut he talken about you know. He say. "The man is right."

"Improvements." I say. "Shitman you can take those improvements. I want a piece I can be sure of. Colt is sure. Lemme ask you somethin Man lemme ask you somethin. Why you think the headbreakers usen a Colt if it no good? Let me ask you that Summer? Man you got Biretta on the brain. You dont have the bread to buy a cap pistol an all you talken is Biretta."

"The Man is right." Handy say. Meanin me. That I am right.

Summer say. "Shitman the reason headbreakers usen the Colt is because they dont know no better. Thats all."

Mister Shapiro he call us over. He tell us not to get lost an stay with the class. Then he say. "Just think boys. This is the place where George Washington tooken the Oath of Office an become our first president."

"Now whut do you think of that." Someone say.

14

Mister Shapiro dont pay no attention to him. He say. "Do you never think boys that they was a time this nation of ours was just one day old?"

"Jus a goddamn baby." Same person say. George Cadmus. Mister Shapiro know but he dont pay any atention. He talken about how rough things was in the old days. Man it was rough at Valley Forge an places like that he tellin us.

Then we walk aroun an look at the sords an things like that from histry an then Mister Shapiro tooken us across the street to the stock exchange. They got these little streets down in that part of town. On one corner they was a man a white man wearin a derby hat tellin a crowd of people about the Bible an they was hecklin him. He was standin on a box with the American Flag painted on it. Some of the guys lit up butts while we was crossin the street an Mister Shapiro made out like he dint notice.

We went into this big bilding then an befor we got on the elevator Mister Shapiro made evrybody throw away his butts. He knew we was smoken. Then we went up to the stock exchange an looked at the exibits about the City of the Future. These rocket ships kept flyin back an forth over it. They were on wires you could see the wires. An the City of the Future it was jus a big housing projeck. If you wanted to know whut it all about they had these phones an you could listen in.

When you picked up the phone you could hear this TV announcer tellin you how much steel they gonna need to bild the City of the Future. George Cadmus was breaken evrybody up. He standen there with the phone saying things like. "Uh huh. You dont say Man. Well uh listen Man how things in Pittsberg?" Like this TV announcer was talken to him.

Then we looked at other exibits about tires an aluminum an then we went inta this big room. We was up on a little balcony an down on the floor these men was running aroun with little bits of paper an yellin like they was a rumble on. Hangin on the wall was the biggest American Flag I ever see any where.

Then it was time for the movie an we all went in to this little movie an saw a movie about America. It show rivers an factories & farms & mountains & a work-inman in a blue shirt buyin stocks. Flash Gordon he was sittin in front of me slash the back of a seat with his blade an all the stuffin started fallin out. An Lonesome Pine unscrewed the arm of his chair with a dime. When the lights went on we made a lot of noise an Mister Shapiro hussled us out an never noticed the damage.

On the way out they give us these little books about

how we could own a Share of America an about how to orginize a club an buy these stocks.

When we got out to the street the bus driver threw his butt away an he say. "All right. This bus was hire for 2 hours an the time is up." An he got in an drive off. Mister Shapiro took us back up town on the subway.

So that was the last day of school an summer started.

Gramma Custis is crazy

Priest stop me in the street. About a week after I went to see him about the piece. He say. "Man I glad to see you. I thinkin sure you was picked up."

"They cant touch me Man."

"You are fast." He say.

"I too fast for em."

"Well I been waiten for you Duke Man. I been sittin up there in my room an waiten. That piece dont rust but it aint gettin any younger."

"I be aroun." I say.

He say. "Un huh. Theys a number of people showin interest in that item. Man you dont want to wait too long."

"I be aroun Priest. I come pick it up in a day or two."

"Plenty of money aroun." Priest say an he lift up

his head an sniff like he was smellin money. "Shouldnt be no trouble for you to raise the bread."

"Aint no trouble." I say. "Listen Man I in a big hurry right now. I see you aroun."

We in front of Hermits restarant. Hermit got 2 big picchers in his window. One of Nasser and one of Nkruma. Hermit a big man in the back to Africa movement. Evry time I go in there he talken about it. I tell him. "Man I dont want to live with lions. It rough enough right here."

Priest say to me. "You need a little cash you can do what Rod do."

"I got other ways." I tell him.

"A couple hours at the Park an you got it made Man."

"I dont go for that." I tell him.

"Easy money Duke. Its easy money."

It make me twitch when people go on talken to me when I dont want to talk. When I get the feelin to move all I want to do is move you know. Like I get this itchyness all over me. In school some time this come over me an I want to start cuttin up an smashin things. You know like they got me an surrouned me an I gotta brake out.

Priest go on talken about the easy money in the Park. I know all about the easy money in the park.

19

Man that kind of action make me feel creepy. He still talken an I say. "Priest I see you tomorra or nex day." An I take off.

"Stay cool." He say.

I walk aroun the block. I dont know what to do. I want some action. When they aint no school it hard to find somethin to do. When school is on it easy to find things to do. Like not goin to school. But in the summer you got to make you own action. I stood on the corner for a while hitten the bus stop sign with my hand. Keeps my hands hardened up. Then I went over to Ritzies Bar lookin for Blood but he wasnt there. Wasnt nobody there but some older guys talkin numbers. "Stay cool." Ritzie say. She give me a big smile. Ritzie she all right. Fine lookin blackskin woman with a lot of hair on top of her head all piled up. She always say. "Look at me Man. I the White Queen of the savages."

I think about how it would be to make it with Ritzie. Walken down the street I think about it. She in her 40s. Maybe 45 like. She a woman with a lot of juice. Late at night. Closin time. I the last one in the bar. She say. "Help me lock up Duke Man." She go in the back room an I lock up and turn off the lights an push the chairs in against the tables. I sit down on a bar stool an wait. Then she call me. I go into the back room. She on the bed all naked her hair spread out on the pilla an her big tits lavishin all over her.

It could happen. I think about Sue Randolph an I say to myself. "Duke go on up see her. Blood dont have to know." So I climb up to her apartment. Halls full of garbage an all kinds of muck and crap. I knock on the door. Her Mother open it. She wearen a flimy robe holden it together with her hand. I say. "Ekscuse me. I guess I knock on the wrong door."

"I guess you goddamn well have knock on the wrong door." She say. "An dont knock on it ever again." She start yellin an I head for the stairs. She yell down after me about keepin my hands off her Sue an like that. I dont like to hear a woman swear. Especially an old woman an a Mother besides.

So then I walk over to Bloods house looken for him. I glad Sue aint home dont want to get hooked by her again. I need whut I need is the kind of woman too old for marryin. Like Ritzie. I sit down on a bench at the project an think about Ritzie again all that thick hot meat. I think if I put my body against hers I get burned by the heat. She make me think if a man put a knife in her she wouldnt stop bleedin for 10 days.

Bloods folks live in the project. His father work for

the Post Office. He been carryin a mail bag so long one shoulder is lower than the other. Blood got one sister a nurse an a brother at Fisk University learning to be a doctor or somethin. Man I dont see it workin they asses off like that. No point workin like that when they can take it all away from you when ever they feel like it you know.

The project has a little elevator like a telephone booth the green walls all scratched with initials an you know things. An it smell like garbage. New bilding but it got the Uptown Stink. It different though inside the Thurston apartment. Evything clean an so neat you afraid to sit down. Missus Thurston she Bloods Mother she open the door an say. "Come on in Richard. John Wesley be right back. I just sent him down to the supermarket." John Wesley. Thats Bloods real name. I go on in.

They must have over a 100 books in they apartment. Missus Thurston say to me. "You remember Harrison dont you Richard. He is home from Fisk." Harrison readin a book. He wearin white shoes with thick red rubber soles dressed like all the College boys. They wear a uniform like they belong to a gang. But they dont belong to no gang.

Harrison look up from his book. "Well Richard." He say. "An how are things goin with you?"

"OK." I say. "How you like it down there at Fisk?"

"Oh we are getting along." He say. "You see a lot of John Wesley dont you Richard?"

"Off an on." I tell him.

Harrison say. "He has changed. I notice a change in him an I am not sure I like it."

Missus Thurston say. "He is like a stranger in this house. As if he did not belong here an was not one of my children."

Harrison say to me. "Have you noticed any change in him lately? You see a lot of him. Has he been doing rather pecular things would you say?"

"He just the same." I say.

Harrison shakin his head. He say to his Mother. "He needs treatment Mother. Thats my opinion. He needs treatment. I do not know what is at the bottom of it but I know somethin is wrong. I wish I could have the head of the Sike Department take a look at him."

After a while an Blood still not back they relize he aint comin back. I knew it all the time. Put some money in Bloods hands he aint goin to no supermarket he goin to the junkman for a fix.

Harrison say to his Mother. "Has he done this sort of thing before Mother?"

She nod.

He say. "Mother have you no idea what is goin on with John Wesley?"

She say. "Oh my GOD Harrison do not be so blind. You brother that poor Lamb he has become an addikt."

Harrison slam his book shut. It go Thuck. He stand up an go to the window an look out. He say to the window. "They make us live like animals. Is it any wunder then that some of us act like animals an some of us become animals. The fantastic thing is how few of us succum to their idea of us." An he went on like that standin there at the window not lookin at us lookin out at Harlem. He a tall skinny boy. He wearen gray slacks with a little buckle in the back an a white shirt.

I get up an say I gotta get on home an if I see John Wesley I tell him they is waiten for him. An I go.

No place to go now but home. Gramma Custis fass asleep in her chair by the window. I go in my mothers room an look thru her draws lookin for some money. I got to buy that piece from Priest. I want it. When you have a gun then you aint no animal any more. You a hunter an can stand tall an dont have to take a soundin from no body.

No money. I lay down on the sofa and lissen to

Gramma Custis snorin. I think about how to get up the bread the $15 I need. I think Maybe I will go to the Park with Rod. Maybe I do it just one or 2 times to get the 15. Or maybe I go look up Chester and borra it from him. He live downtown now an is doin all right. Then I start thinkin about Ritzie again so I get up an start walkin aroun. I go to the closet an look in the pockets of every piece of clothes. Nothin. At the back of the closet I see the shoe shine box I uset to lug aroun when I was a kid to pick up pennies shinin shoes. I give it a kick. Dont know why I aint ever throw it out. The stink of shoe polish is the worse stink of all.

When I kick the box Gramma Custis mumbel in her sleep. I look at her. She dont wake up. She got her big black leather purse on the floor near her feet. She always keep her Welfare money in it. She fold the foldin money inta little squares an stuff them inta a little purse like the money gonna last longer that way.

No body ever know how much she got. I walk over to the window an pretend I lookin out but I lookin at her. She still snorin. I kneel down an open her purse. It got a little gold clasp. I squeeze it real tight so it wont make no sound. When it open I look up at her. Her eyes is closed and her face all sagged. I reach inside for the little purse but alla time I keep watchin

Gramma. When my hand touches the little purse I stop breathin. Then I look down and open it. They maybe 20 little squares of $1 bills inside.

"You boy!"

I drop the purse an stan up fast. I tryin so hard to preten I wasnt doin nothing that I believe it myself.

She glarin at me thru her glasses. She say. "Steelin from you own Gramma. Oh GOD whut gonna become of you boy. Whut happenin to you Richard you was the sweetest baby so good. An now you is so bad. Whut happenen to you."

I dint say nothin. She lean tord me in her chair like she goin to poke me. She say. "It the city. It this city this hore of Babylon. This hore city is whut happenin to you makin you go bad that was so sweet an good. This here place is the seat of Satan an it bringen you to ruin an damnation. An I will kill her childern with death The Bibel say. You a child of Babylon. An upon her forhead was a name written. MYSTERY. BABYLON THE GREAT. THE MOTHER OF HARLOTS AN ABOMINATIONS OF THE EARTH. An the woman which thou sawist is that great city which raineth over the kings of the earth." She say.

"I aint been anywheres near Ritzies Bar." I tell her. But she dont listen.

She say. "Babylon Babylon Babylon the great is

fallen boy. Is fallen. An is become the habitation of debles. An the hold of evry fowl speerit. An a cage of evry unclean an hateful bird. For all nations have drunk of the wine of the wrath of her fornication. An the kings of the earth have committed fornication with her. An the merchants are waxen rich off a her delicacies."

She stop for a minute an I say. "I just been over to the Thurstons. They boy Harrison is home now from Fisk University."

"Harrison is a good boy." She say. "He a credit to the Race. Come out of her my people that you be not partakers of her sin."

She off again. She say. "Come out of Babylon so that you dont receive of her playgs. Therefore shall her playgs come in one day. You lissen to me boy. Death an mornin & famine & she shall be utterly burned with fire."

"Yes Mam." I say.

"You shall see the smoke of her burning boy. Alla you liven deliciously with her an committin fornication with her you gonna bewail when you see the smoke." She point out the window. "Standin afar off for the fear of her torment." She say. "Sayin alas alas that mighty city Babylon. For in 1 hour is thy judgment come. An the merchants of the earth is gonna weep because they cant buyeth they merchandise no more. Cinamon and frankisense an horses & slaves & pearls. Ointmints & oil & wheat & fine linen. Thou shalt find them no more at all boy. In one hour boy it gonna happen. In 1 hour she gonna be made desolate. GOD aint gonna over look it for ever boy. You watch out. The angel gonna throw the millstone and he sayith thus with vilence shall that great city Babylon be thrown down. For thy merchants were the great men of earth an by thy sorceries were all nations deceeved." Her face all streaky an wet with cryin. "You own Gramma." She say. She say. "Oh that sweet little lovenable boy whut happen to him. Where he gone?"

The super is king

One time 3 Wolves japped me in my own bilding. That was in the time when I uset to go evry night to Sue Randolph when her mother was workin nights. First I uset to go there right after school but then Sue mother start workin nights so I go there nights. After a while of this Blood say to me—Blood is President of the Crocadiles—Blood say to me. "Duke Man you gotta make up you know you gotta make up you mind like. You wanta like bang this this girl evry night or you gonna swing with us. Ever since you start gettin in on Sue we aint see you aroun here hardly at all."

"Shitman." I say.

"That the truth Duke. We dont hardly see you no more. You out for ass *all* the time Man?"

"I still with the gang Blood." I tell him.

"I sure glad to hear that Duke. I truly glad. You got heart Man an we like need you you know."

He look me up and down. Then he say. "You know Man uh uh uh since he got so bad beat up by the cops Little Man aint much good to us. I been thinkin of puttin you in his slot Man. Makin you War Lord." He smile his big crazy smile. His face aint nothin but teeth when he smile. Bloods real name is John Wesley but no body call him that anymore. "How you like that Man?" He ask me.

So I stopped goin to Sue Randolph.

But at this time I tellin you about I still goin there evry night till 2-3 o'clock in the mornin. I feelin good. Struttin down the street like a hot shot. Struttin like a numbers man with a big bank. Thinkin of Sue up there stretched out on the bed smilin an sayin. "Duke you good to me I be good to you Lover. You good to me I be good to you. Dont you ever leave me Duke. Hear? Dont leave me Duke. Be good to me an I be good for you." An things like that.

So I walkin home like a hotshot but lookin allatime right left in evry doorway. Closer I get to my house the more I get a feelin. I get a feelin they are out and waiten. First I think Maybe it will be at the hardware store. An I come up on my toes. Walkin soft. Blade in my hand. I am cool. I am cool. Man but my goddamn heart wont stop poundin. I can hear it in my ears. "Oh you motheren heart." I say. Times like that you know you say crazy things. Oh you motheren heart. Then I say. Motheren Wolves. Motheren Wolves. Come at me you Motherens.

Thought I seen shadows movin. In the doorway between the two windas. I walk with eyes in the side of my head Man. Comin up on them. Slow. Slow & quiet. Only my goddam heart. I move in close to the bilding so I have my back against it when they rush me.

But they wasnt there at the hardware store. Wasnt they. Wasnt nothin there but two windos fulla E Z Kill roach powder and Kill Kwik rat pellets & a big picktcher of a dead rat. I stop there for a minute in the doorway an get my self unsweated.

I sure they aroun. I can smell Wolves. I can feel when the street get a certain kind of quiet you know or it got a kind of *feel*. Then I know the Wolves is out standin in some dark door with the blades in they hands or maybe one of them has a piece is holdin it ready to shoot up. Step out sudden an say to me. "Where you think you goin nigger?"

Only one more place they can be layin for me—in the door in the Church of the Black Jesus. Big store winda with a hand painted pictcher of Jesus sayin

Come Unto Me an 3 runty lams. He dressed in a sheet wearin crazy white hair.

I put my back to the winda. I smell Wolves sure this time an I have the blade in my hand open an ready. Motherens. Come at me you motherens. I take a quick look in the doorway. Whish! With my head an whish! right back. Fast. Did not see no body. Slower this time. Easy. I put one eye aroun. No body. I laugh. I say. "Duke you smell Wolves but they aint none. You smeller gone bad." I laugh and put my blade away.

Then I walk 2 more doors an up the steps an in to my bilding. An the door close behin me too fast. The light is out. An I knowed all at once the Wolves was there in my own bilding. Wolves. Oh shitman. An I run for it in to the dark hall tryin to make the stairs. But they on me. 3 of them. An I get in only 1 good one. My fist hit somethin soft an it make that nice rippin sound like somethin tare.

They come at me they come at me with they blades the motherens & I throw up my arms for protection over my face and go into a crouch. They cut up my arms somethin bad.

Too dark to see they faces an see who it is. It black dark and I cant hear only they breathin and the shuffelen of shoes. I feel the blood trickilin down my arms. Then I hear a Wolve say. "Get his arms down Man. Get the bastards arms down. I gonna mark his face that hotshot Duke."

I know what is comin so I try to rush them & break through but they have the blades on me & throw me back against the wall & then they kick me in the belly. I try to stand but it bend me over an they get to my face. Little Angel it was probly. An he mark me on the cheek.

I start goin down. An just then Mister Hurst appear outa no where. Suddenly he just there loomin up all over the hall. Mister Hurst he the super lives in the basemint and carries out the garbage cans like they was filled with nuthin. He hardly ever talk. He sets on the stoop an puffs his pipe an he got shoulders and hands on him like a heavywait.

He pick up those 3 Wolves blades an all an heave them out the door. I went down. Head on the dirty floor in my own blood. I seen Mister Hurst throw em out. It was Little Angel all right. I reckonized him when he hit the street. He hit the street an took off without losin time . Little Angel is fast Man but I am faster. I am the fastest.

Mister Hurst carry me up the 5 flights. My collar was wet with the blood. "Them motheren Wolves." I say to Mister Hurst.

"They are just poor boys like you." He say. "Wolves. They aint no Wolves." His voice boom in his chest like a big cannon. I hear it boomin in my ears and right thru my skull.

"Dear Jesus they bringin my Richard home in blood again." My mother say when she open the door.

The super he carry me in the front door & put me on the sofa. When my mother turn on the light she say. "Sweet Jesus. O sweet Jesus Lord." Then she say to Mister Hurst. "You think he need a docter?"

Mister Hurst he tell her. "This boy need all the docters in the world."

He went away an mother she wash up my face and arms & put on some banages. Gramma Custis woke up and come in her hair in white ropes and prayed Sweet Jesus guide our boy an crap like that you know. My mother tell me. "Richard you go on like this you come to a bad end sure."

I went to sleep and dreamed Mister Hurst was King of the Negroes. He in a gold tent settin on a gold throne like & we carry him down Park Avenue to 96th Street & then cut over to 5th Avenue and back up town again. Bands playin in uniforms & fire engines & a million people wavin flags. People yellin. "Mister Hurst is our King. Mister Hurst is our King." An we all singin and dancin up the street throwin Kwik

Kill pellets in the air. People cryin an shoutin. "We have our own. Man we have our own at last." Mister Hurst sittin there on the gold throne puffin his pipe. Kwik Kill pellet falls on his platform he just stick out his foot easy like an brush it off. People sayin. "O Man. O Man. O Man."

When I wake up it still dark an I hear my mother talkin to her husband about me. They in bed in the next room.

"No good worryin." He tell her.

"I know it."

"No good at all."

"I know it." She say. 'But I just cant help worryin."

"Wont do no good."

"He my one & only child."

"Forget it now honey."

"He all I got."

"Ho now." He say.

She laugh. "I aint forgettin about you *Mister* Osborne. You dont *let* me forget about you."

They both laugh then. "Ah Christ." He say. "This the only good thing they left us in life. Jesus." He say. "Jesus woman you sweet all ovuh."

When I wake up I hear it is Sunday. The loud speaker from in front of the church is soundin off.

35

Church where I thought the Wolves was hidin. My face feel all tight from the cut on my cheek.

Preacher blarin out on the loud speaker. "Ah tell you brothers an Ah tell you sisters it is the most important & pressin question before us. It been hangin over the white Christians 10-15 centuries now. Was Christ Our Dear Lord a white man or a black man? That is the question! An whut is the answer? Whut is the answer Sister & Brothers?—As a matter of fack & to be exack Our Lord & Savior Christ was black!"

Gramma Custis settin by the window noddin her head. "It the truth." She say. "It the truth. We all know it the truth. Dont the Bibel say he was a Lions Whelp. Apostle Paul say He sprung outa *Judah!* He were *black!* They aint no single solitary doubt of that. O Sweet Jesus Baby make youself plain and clear to the white folk. Show em you is with us & of us once & for all."

An she went on like that you know. Man like anybody cared.

Lu Ann

Befor the cops beat him so bad on the head Little Man
uset to be War Lord of the Crocadiles. Man he had
heart. One time he stood up by him self against 6
Wolves. He got pick up by the cops and dint have the
chance to get rid of his piece. It was a zip gun he made
in shop. Little Man so sly an wise he made that piece
in shop right under the teachers nose. Mister Swen-
lund the teachers name.

When Little Man got home from the precinct he
tell us. "Them headbreakers. Motheren headbreakers
—3 of em beatin up on me hittin me on the head all
the time with their goddam fists. You give us too
much trouble you little black bastard. Wham. Sock.
Wham. One in front of me. Put up my hands to
protect myself. Wham they hit me from the back.
Bend ovuh they hit me from the side. 3 of em. Teach

37

you a little lesson black boy. Murderer. This here detective sets there. He dont hit me. He just keep wipin his shoes on my suit. Make me so mad I wanta kill him." Little Man slam his fist into the wall. He dont even feel it. His head buzzin and roarin allatime he say.

When he get home his father waiten for him. "You gonna end up like you brother." He say. "You gonna end up just like you brother. I am glad you mother dead an not here to see the shame. You gonna end up just like you brother." An evrytime he say it he kick Little Man. That all he know how to do. Kick.

Little Man start screamin. He go for his father with the bread knife. His father pick up a chair and hold him off. Little Man screamin allatime an his father cryin. "You own father. Kill you own father. You gonna end up like you brother. Just like him. That the way you gonna end up." Few days later the old man pack up an leave. He dont say a word to Little Man. He just go.

"I glad he gone." Little Man say.

Blood tell him. "Things is bad all over Little Man."

"Who need him?" Little Man say. "All he know how to do is kick. No bettern a cop."

"Man uh uh uh its tough." Blood say. He say.

38

"Little Man. Tell you whut we gonna do. We need a place like. A club house you know. Now how bout this listen to this for an idee. We all pay dues. Dues pay the rent. You stay here and go on livin here like it was you house an we come use it for a club house Man. No more hangin out at Louies Place and gettin picked on by the bulls allatime. We come here. Got a nice secret place."

"That great Blood." Evrybody say. "You got it Man." They say. "This is whut we need."

Little Man say. "OK with me Blood. But Edison already turn off the lights."

"Leave em off." Blood say. "Leave em off Man. Who need it? We gonna buy candles this place gonna look real spooky an nice."

So evrybody in the Crocadiles gets up a dollar a month and we got ourselves a sweet place Man. Crocadiles dont hang out in some cellar like the Wolves. We got ourselves a place. Inside toilet and evrything.

One day Blood come in with this girl with him. She look about 15. Skinny an wearen a real tight dress. Lu Ann her name.

Blood say. "Boys this here Lu Ann."

Lu Ann say. "Hi." An she look at us one by one like it a line up. Then she look around our club house. "Nice little spread you got youself Boys." She say.

39

Blood take her in the room with the big bed where Little Mans father uset to sleep. About 12 of us sittin there in the kitchen. Me & Little Man. Fortyfive. Big Jeff. Cowboy. Rod an all.

Cowboy look at me. I say. "Keep cool Man."

Then Blood come in. He sets down and put his feet on the table. He smile an say. "Man this is livin."

"Whut about the chick?" Cowboy ask him.

"Yeh." Rod say.

I say. "We goin Social? Aint we a fightin club no more?"

"Cool Man." Blood say. "Stay cool and lissen to me. The Crocadiles aint goin Social. We a fightin club. Now this chick . . ."

"Who this Lu Ann Chick?"

"That whut Im tellin you." Blood say. "Now evry gang thats big uh uh uh really big you know why its got a girl of its own."

"The Bishops had one." Rod say.

"Now this girl this Lu Ann." Blood say. "She aint no neiborhood kid."

"Whut you mean?" Cowboy say.

"I mean she a pro. She been getting paid for it for a year now."

"That kid?" Rod say.

Cowboy say. "I believe it Man. She got the stuff."

"Nothin but bones." Rod say.

"Sweet meat on the hoof." Cowboy say an he lick his lips. Evrybody laugh.

"Wait a minute." Blood say holdin up his big hand. Cowboy sit down. "Jus one minit. Like I say Lu Ann is the Crocadile whore she our own property exclusive."

"But." Rod say.

"But." Blood say. "You gotta pay the up keep on the property." He laugh his crazy big laugh an his eyes slide aroun in his head. "She dont put out for nobody but Crocadiles hear? Now it gonna cost evrytime you jump her."

"How much?" Cowboy want to know.

Blood look at him. "Stay cool Man." Then he wait a little to see if Cowboy under his thumb. Cowboy dont say nothin. Blood say. "One dollar fifty. One dollar for Lu Ann and 50 cents for the treasury. 50 cents is the club cut. You guys do enough humpin we have enough money soon to buy some pieces."

"We don need pieces to go down on the Wolves." Rod say. "We still waitin to revenge em for whut they done to Duke."

"Aint this a fightin club no more?" Mission say.

Blood look aroun at evrybody. Flickin his eyes on evry face. "Whuts this?" He say. He puts both his

41

hands on the table. "Now lissena me." He say. "Lissen an get it straight for I dont want to go on repeatin this for ever. The headbreakers are out there thickerin flies. Things is hot like they never been befor. Soons things cool off we go down on the Wolves and bust em. We gonna kill em an destroy em." His hands start shakin and they is spit on his lips and chin. "We gonna leave em splash all over the goddam street those motherens." He pick up his hand an slam it on the table. Big as a ham that hand of Bloods. "We gonna smash em. But we gonna smash when I say smash. Hear?" Then he get up and walk to the door his eyes all creamy like you know. At the door. He say. "Take care of Lu Ann & don forget—1 dollar on the bed an 50 cents in the box."

"Dont you want any of it Blood?" Mission ask.

Blood laugh. "Maybe I gonna come back when it all warm up for me."

Cowboy say. "Well who is gonna start the action?"

Evrybody laugh.

Cowboy laugh too. "Well I guess it up to me." He say an walks into the room where Lu Ann is.

The guys that dont have the bread get up and start leavin. Mission go out the door sayin. "I don have to pay for it." But Man I dont know why it is. You dont feel like a man till you leave some money on the bed.

Biggest man on the street

When I come down stairs from Lu Ann Rod waiten
for me on the stoop. He looken troubled.

"Rod Man you look like you got somethin on you
mind." I say.

"That Blood." He say.

I sit down with him an put my han on his shoulder.

"Blood is on the junk." He say. "I wasnt sure befor
tonight but tonight I am sure."

"He on the junk all right." I say.

Rod look at me.

"He been on it 4-5 week I know of." I say. "I can
always spot the junkies."

"You an Officer of the Crocadiles. Man you should
of done somethin about it." He say.

When a guy is takin H he got to get outa the gang.

That a law. You cant rely on a junkie an they can get a gang inta a lot of trouble.

Rod say. "We shoulda gone down on the Wolves right away after they beat up on you. We shoulda revenged you. All Blood want is money to buy his stuff. That all he care about. Bringin that girl here an all you know. It for the money."

"He aint gonna get no money out of it." I say to Rod.

"He gonna get it Duke. He jus gonna dip inta the box an take it. Junkies dont care. When they need the stuff they sell they goddam shoes an close. Or steal. Steal anything aint nailed down. My Father done it. They all do it."

"Im gonna watch him Rod."

"We should throw him out right now Man." Rod say. He all shook up.

"Blood a big Man. He got a Rep. Evrybody in this territory is scared of him." I say to Rod.

"You cant watch him all the time. He steal the money we have to beat up on him an *then* throw him out. Save a lot of trouble to throw him out right now."

"When the time come Rod I gonna take care of Blood myself." I tell Rod. I got heart. I got a Rep.

"I know it." Rod say. "Duke man you got heart an

44

you got brains. I like to see you President when we get rid of Blood."

"Shitman."

"That the truth Man." Rod say. "You the best for the job." Rod start hoppin up an down. He say. "Then we start boppin again. Break a few heads & cut up them Wolves. Oh Man oh shitman how I hate them motherens. How I hate. We been layin off too long. I got the resslessness. I wanta get my matchete an go cuttin again. Eeeee Christ Man I don like this sittin aroun."

"Easy Man. Stay cool."

"I mean it Duke. I don like it. It like the old days when Warrior was President and we had the girls auxillary."

"We did a lot of boppin in those days."

"Them girls in an out all the time." Rod say. "They jus aint no place in a gang for girls. You buy the piece from Priest yet?" He ask me.

"Not yet Man. Man it hard to get up the bread."

"You go see Royal Baron like I tol you?"

"I goin to see him soon Rod. I been busy with some other little things."

"You go see him." Rod say. "I tol him you is a good man."

"He still at the same place?"

"Yeh. Things has cooled off."

"Well I go see him real soon Rod."

"Pick up the bread easy that way Duke. You gonna need that piece. Nobody push you when you got a piece. Anybody sound you—bam. Bam bam. Put holes in em." He look at me smilin. "You know whut Id like Duke? You know whut? I wanta get me a rifle with tele scopic sights an a box of ammo an lay out on the roof. Jus you know *be* there with it an kill people walkin down in the street. Bam. An they dead with out known it. No body ever catch me. Man I wanta be the Black Death an live on the roof & bam put holes in em. Kill an disapeer. Special hidin place for my rifle an the tele scopic sights. Cops never find it. Goddam headbreakers." He put his hand on my arm. "That is whut I wanta do Duke. Man when you President of the Club I gonna change my name. Black Death. Black Death. That whut I wanta be called."

"That a good name." I tell him.

He stan up sudden like. "Lets go to the Park an look for Wolves. Duke Man I feel like boppin tonight."

"Man it too late for the Park. Aint no body there now but the headbreakers."

"That so." He say. "You smart Duke. I forgot

whut time of night it is. Maybe I go over to Ritzies Bar an drink some wine."

"Like to go with you Death but I got a little job to do."

He smile big when he hear me call him Death. "I with you Duke Man." He say. "Whut ever you decide is gonna be all right with me."

He went off to Ritzies then & I cross the street an took up position. I stood in a door way in a shadow an I watch the door of Little Mans bilding. In a while they all come down. Cowboy first. He stand there on the stoop rockin on his heels real cool like but he lookin left & right. He dont see me. He give a little wiggle with his hand an the others come out. They all look left an right too. Then they go struttin down the street feelin good cause they all together. All Royal Crocadiles. They good men. I wait a little while more. Then I move.

I go up fast. I put the key in the lock with out a sound hopin they aint put on the chain an the bolt. Door opens. I smile an lick my lips. Dark inside. I move thru the kitchen inta the bed room. Little Man & Lu Ann fast asleep in the big bed. Lu Ann naked. Little Man wearin a shirt an makin cryin sounds in his sleep.

I reach out to touch Lu Ann but before I can touch

her she say. "You come back for more Honey?" She tell me Little Man in the bed because he lonely an want company.

"Come in the kitchen." I tell her.

I went in an lit the candle an got the jug of wine from where Blood an I hid it. She come in with nothin on. "Man it hot in here." She say. She see the wine an laugh out loud. "Crazy Man. Whut I need." An she drink down a big glass of it. "I din expec you back so soon Duke." She laugh again. "You mus be a rich man Duke."

I dont tell her I got ony but 30 cents. I fill up her glass again an she drink it.

"How old you now Lu Ann?" I ask her.

"18" She say.

I laugh at her. She laugh an say. "I be 16 soon. You afraid of jail bait Big Man?"

"I aint afraid of nothin." I tell her.

She sit herself on my lap. She say. "I wasnt soundin you Duke Honey. I know you aint afraid of nothin. You the biggest man aroun here. I glad you come back Duke." She say. She got pointy little tits like knuckles. "It lonely here with jus that crazy Little Man."

"Little Man got beat up bad by the cops." I tell her.

"I aint blamin *him*." She say. "I aint blamin him

48

Duke. I know he cant help it. You ever kill any cops Duke?"

She talkin in my ear & I can smell the wine from her mouth. "Not yet I aint killed any. But I buyin a piece tomorrow or next day." She got a tight little ass. My one hand almos cover it.

"Any time Duke. Anytime Duke you want me to hide you piece you jus bring it to me an I hide it no headbreaker ever find it."

"You all right Lu Ann." I say. I look at her.

She say. "You got the money Duke? Blood say—"

"I got it all right." I tell her.

"You dont happen to have any reefers on you Duke? I like to get a couple for the mornin." She say.

I tell her. "I don happen to have any on me right now. I bring you some first thing tomorra."

She laugh. "You got a busy day tomorra Man. I better fix you up good tonight."

"Lets go in the front room." I say. "We use Little Mans bed."

"I like a big bed Duke."

"Let him sleep. We do all right up front in the little bed."

"OK Duke." She say. "You gimme the money now."

"I give it to you." I tell her.

"Now." She say.

I carry her inta the front room. She dont way hardly nothin at all an I throw her down on the bed. Then she put her hans between her legs you know. She say. "If you dont have it all Duke if you dont have the full one dollar fifty then how much *have* you got?"

I take the 3 dimes from my pocket an drop em on her belly. She still don take her hans away. She lift her head a little from the pillow an look down at the money. "You cant get hardly nothin for that Man." She say. Then she look up at the ceelin an pretend like she considerin. She say. "Lets see now Man whut I can give you for that."

I take off my shirt an pants.

"Jus wastin you time." She say.

I don say a word. Jus look at her.

"Spose Blood come back." She say.

I say. "Blood better not come back."

She look at me.

"You hear me." I say. "As of here & now Blood is the X President of the Crocadiles."

"You kill him Duke?" She ask me.

"Take you hans outa there & pick up the money." I tell her. I get on the bed an kneel there lookin down at her. "Get you hans outa there." I say.

"I don give away nothin." She say.

I slap her acrost the face. Two good ones left & right. She spit at me an bring her legs up to kick & I slam her in the belly. That open her up. She lay they tryin to get her breath. "You motheren." She say. I slap her again. It funny you know. You beat up on a skinny little girl an it make you feel more like a Man than standin up by youself to 3 Wolves.

"You really the new chief Duke?" She ask me.

"You heard me."

"You wont forget to bring me the reefers first thing tomorra?"

"I be here with em befor you are awake." I say.

"Then OK Duke." She say. "Give it to me good Man." She say. "You strong Duke. Christ you the strongest. Man Christ you big Duke. You gonna be the biggest Man on the street Duke." Then she make all those you know moans and sounds like whores do. They all do it. Seems like the same person teach em all.

The time the old woman got eat by the dog

I dreamed about goin to the Zoo when I was a little kid. One of my mothers husbands carried me on his shoulders an I was eatin pop corn an some of it spillin down on his head. He look up an smile at me but when I wake up I can never remember his face. When ever I try to remember as far back as I can remember this is whut I remember. But I dont know who he was or his name or anything. I just remember at the Zoo on this mans shoulders eatin pop corn. An the lion behind bars.

I got up early because I had a lot to do. My mother was drinkin coffee in the kitchen. She work days now in a laundry. I come in an pour myself a cup of coffee an eat 5-6 slices of bread with it. My mother sittin there all hunched up over her cup.

"Why you up so early today? I worry so when you

get up so early. Gives you more time for you to get youself in trouble. You aint but 14 now an already you full of scars an stitches. I dont have the strenth to take care of you an look after you like I should." An like that.

"I be all right." I tell her.

"Some time I sorry I ever lef Alabama an lef you with Gramma Custis those years. When I come up here for the opportunities. An then I come back down an brought you up here. Aint never anythin been right since."

I ask her. "Whut was the name of that husband who took me to the zoo when I was a little kid?"

She look up at me again. "Whut took you to the Zoo?"

"When I was a little kid he took me to the Zoo an I ride on his shoulders."

"I dont remember any of that Richard."

"He bought me pop corn."

"Maybe it was George Dickinson." She say. "Or maybe it was befor that. Maybe it was Hillard. Hillard always like you. Some times he play with you."

"Whut was his last name?"

"Jackson." She say. "Jackson. Or Johnson. Why you wanta know?"

"Maybe I meet him someday. I dont know."

She laugh. "You wont be meetin Hillard. Dont you worry bout that." She get up to leave. "You lose a person in Harlem you never see him again. Any man get adrift in Harlem he sink outa sight for ever." At the door she say. "Now you stay outa trouble today Richard here? For if you get inta trouble again I dont know I swear I dont know whut I gonna do cept beat you good. You get in trouble once more I washen my hans of you. You gonna have to make out by youself best way you know how. I dont have the strenth no more. You dont know whut it like all day standin in that steam an the wet. An the turrible ache in my bones. It a shame to GOD to make a woman work so an then they go an take all that money outa my pay for the taxes an this & that & the other thing. Whut they want taxes from me for when they never give me nothin? No. Nothin. But this. Roaches & rats. Roaches & rats. Aint nothin decent in our lives. I ony wanted but the one husband you father but things got too much for him an he ran off an lef me. Things always get too much for men. They thinkin all day of whut they comin home to an one time they jus don come home. It easy for them. You a man an you jus like the others. All of you is a like. You ony know how to give a woman sadness an cause her pain an suffrin. You get in trouble jus one more time an I

54

turnin you over to the cops. This time I tell the Judge and the Youth People—Take him. Take him he aint none of mine—I dont want have anythin further to do with this boy." An like that you know.

I drink my coffee an not look at her.

She yell. "You hear me Richard you damn boy you?"

"I hear you." I say.

She leave. Slams the door so loud all the dogs in the bilding start barkin an keep on barkin all the way down the stairs. She take the subway to Queens now an be home 6-30 or 7 o'clock. After my mother leave I drink another cup of coffee an when Gramma Custis come in with the Bibel in her han I clear out.

She say. "Where you goin boy?"

I slam the door an the dogs start barkin again.

When I turn the turn of the stairs at the 2nd floor I see 2 men in uniform an I pull back quick. Not even breathin. Then I realize they aint cops by they uniforms an I step down the last step inta the hall. Door is open at Missus Jeffersons apartment. She an old old woman whut lives alone with a big mean dog. Stretcher leanin against the wall. Inside is 2 men with a net tryin to catch the dog. Dog makin a crazy sound in his throat an you can smell him out in the hall. I so busy watchin them at first I dint notice Missus Jefferson layin on the floor an whut she look like. When I get a look at her I run downstairs.

Lot of people on the stoop. One woman sayin. "She layin they dead 2-3 days. Oh I knowed I shoulda look in on her. An that dog—an she love that dog so —treated him like a little baby—that dog got so hungry he et her."

The men come out with that dog snappin and strugglin in the net. Everybody stan back an the woman say. "You a bad bad dog." The men put him in the back of a truck marked society against the cruelty to animals or somethin like that an they drive off with the dog.

Then the stretcher men come down with Missus Jefferson. They got a blanket coverin her.

The woman say. "Good by Mamie you sweet soul." She cryin.

The man take off his hat an open the door of the dead wagon for the stretcher men. He say to them. "Scratch one nigger more." The men dont say any thing. They drive away.

I walk up to 125 street to see Royal Baron.

Poinciana Co.

Royal Baron had the chain on the door. When he open it I see one eye. A sign on the door in gold letter say POINCIANA CO.

"Yas?" Royal Baron say thru the slot. "Whut is it you want Son?"

"Duke Custis my name." I say.

The mouth smile an he take off the chain an open the door. "Yas. Come in Lad." He say. An I go in. "Rod has spoke highly of you Lad."

I folla him in to a parlor where they is a big desk a sofa & some chairs. He go aroun behind this big desk an he sit down. On the desk they is a phone with buttons on it & about 29 ball point pens. "Sit down Lad." He say.

I sit down on a chair near his desk. He lean back in a swibel chair & look at me. Then he say. "I like a

Lad who get up bright an early an start de day wit de sun." He from the West Indys an he talk like that. Real crazy like.

He say. "This here Company that I have foundit—The Poinciana Co.—is in a state of high expansion right now at this moment. You come here at a good time Lad. My company if I say so myself is one of the leaders in the field. If you got the grit boy and if you got the determination you can rise with us. No limit to the possibilities Lad. I long ago discovered Lad that if you think Money all the time day & night without stopping—Money will come to you. Money will love you. Do you love Money Lad?"

I say. "Yes sir I love Money. I like to make 35-40 a week."

"Yas." He say. "An Lad you can do it with me. I give you as an example the case of Bobby X. Bobby came to me a year ago. A poor boy off the streets. Lackin all the amenity of home and lovin parents. I took him into my organization an give him a start as Sales Man. Today that boy has an apartment of his own. He has a 1957 Chevrolay an many friends of both sexes."

He stop talken like he waitin for me to say somethin. I say. "Is that the fella whut works on a hundred 16th street?"

"I dont divulge things Lad." He say. "That is one thing you will soon discover about me if we mutually decide on you entering this here organization." He lift up his hand like he taken the Oath in court. He say. "They can beat me with the clubs. They can beat me with the hoses. Royal Baron dont divulge."

Bed room door open an a blonde chick step out. She dressed in one of those pink things like in a picktcher in Confidential Magazine. She dont see me right away an she say to Royal Baron. "Mornin Roy Honey."

Royal Baron look over at me. He say. "Uh. Uh."

She see me then. "Good mornin Mister Baron." She say.

He say. "This is my secretary Miss Dewpont. This Lad here may be joinin our orginization Miss Dewpont."

She give me a big smile. "That will be real nice." She say.

"I have some dictation for you in a little while." Baron say to her. She go in the kitchen & pretty soon I smell the coffee cookin.

Royal Baron put his fingers on his eyes like they hurtin him. Then he say. "Now lets see. Where was we? Oh yas. As I was sayin Lad this here business is growin by leaps an bounds an my lookout is to see that I continues to get my fair share. The problem the big problem is one of distribution. As Henry Ford the old man once said—The engineers can solve every problem but the problem of distribution. An thats the truth Lad. Thats the truth. My hardest job is to find good trust worthy young men like you will turn out to be I hope an fondly trust. Young men who want to rise and make somethin out of them selves."

He lean back in the chair an rub his eyes again. He swibel aroun an look out the window like he gonna talk to it. Then he do talk to it. Like I aint even aroun. He say to the window. "I have the fond hope that some day when we get men of intelligence an probity down in Washington this business will be legalized. Yas." He say. "But unfortunately Lad they is but slim hope of that."

He stan up an start walkin up & down the room with his hands behin his back. "But I live in hope Lad." He say. "I live an hope. If this business was legal I be millionair in no time at all. A *multy* million-air."

Miss Dewpont come in with a cup of coffee an a donut. She all blonde. A white woman. She sit down near me an put her cup on the arm of her chair. She catch my eye an smile at me an then she open her mouth an bit into the donut.

Royal Baron say. "Oh if we was legal Lad. If ony we was legal like the other cigarette companies. Evry year Id plow back one percent of the gross inta advertising. Put on a big campaign. Posters in the subway. Girl sittin in a swing—lot of flowers an things aroun her indicatin she is accustom to the better things life offers—an under it it say—I smoke Poincianas."

"That would be real lovely Roy." Miss Dewpont say lookin at me.

Royal Baron say. "Answer me this Lad. You ever hear any of my customers complain they got any cancer or other malignacy from smokin Poincianas?"

"No sir." I say.

"You damn right Lad." He say. "Never a complaint. Not one. 10 Years in the business off & on an not one recorded case of cancer or other malignacy laid at the door of the Poinciana Co. Now I ask you this Lad—can any other of those cigarette cos. make that claim?"

"No sir." I say.

"You damn right Lad." He say. He all shook up about it. He walk aroun the room. He say. "They cant lay no claim to producin a harmless product. Where as the Poinciana Co. can. Our product gives pleasure. Real pleasure. It is non habit forming & has no harmful after effects. Are you a user Lad?"

61

"Off & on." I tell him.

"I glad of that." He say. "I prefer that my Sales Men be users of the product." He say. "A satisfied customer is our best advertisement."

"That a real nice sentiment Roy." Miss Dewpont say. "Lovely."

Royal Baron put his hand on my shoulder. He say. "Let me show you around the shop Lad. This here in here is the administrative offices."

I stand up an folla him. "We leavin the administrative offices now an enterin the factory proper."

We go thru the kitchen an then into a small room. They was 2 women workin at a table with a glass top. Piles of tobaca on the table an these women take little pinches of it an stick it inta little white envelopes. They work fast. They fingers flickin in an out.

"This here the factory proper." Royal Baron say. Then he say to the 2 women. "Good Mornin Ladies."

"Mornin Mister Baron." They say.

One of these women got grey hair tied in a knot at the back of her head an I reckanize her. Missus Byrd. From my neighborhood. She a big churchwoman like my Gramma.

Royal Baron say. "This here young Lad may be joinin our organization."

The 2 old ladies they smile at me but they hands

keep movin flick flick. In & out of the tobaco. Inta the envelopes. Back to the tobaco again. Missus Byrd say to me. "Aint you Mamie Custis granson?"

"Yes mam." I say.

"I thought so." Missus Byrd say. She smile. "She a good woman Mamie Custis is. An if you her granson I know you must be a good boy. I sure you gonna contribit some of you earned money to you mother that hard workin soul may GOD bless her."

"Yes mam." I say.

"GOD will bless you for it." She say.

Royal Baron say. "I glad to hear this Lad is of good family. Lets return now to the administrative offices."

Miss Dewpont gone. Royal Baron sit down at his desk. He pick up a ball point an click it open & shut a few times. Then he put it down an rub his eyes like they hurtin again.

Then he say. "I aint gonna go inta the cost & price structure in any great detail Lad. My accountant tell me he dont see how I can continue rewardin my Sales Staff so hansomely. But I say to him—my Sales Men are the life blood of the bizness Harrison. They my front line troops & even if it mean goin without for my self I am goin to do right by them. I gonna start you out to day with 12 packets. The price to the consumer is $1 per each. Your commission Lad is 25¢.

Thats high reward Lad for the little work an the small hardly mentionable risk involved. Name me another corporation that rewards its Sales Men so hansomly. I am prepared to match it penny for penny. Name me one." He say an he hit the desk with his hand.

I just sit there.

"In deed you cant name me one." He say. He all shook up. "An this is only the beginin Lad." He say. "I look forward to the time when there be men of vision in Washington & I can provide my Staff with the Blue Cross & vacations with pay & retirement plan for the declinin years. An all other benefits." He say. "But things bein how they are all I can do is give you money so as you can live good today an provide for an old age of security an comfort."

"Yes sir." I never know whut to say to him. All them West Indy Negroes is a like. They all half crazy with bein English.

"You think you can sell 12 a day?" He ask me. "As a start Lad. I mean as a start. After a while you build up you custom they aint they no limit to the sales potential. You just sit in you apartment or you car or you favorite cafe after a while & the customers come to you. I talken now as of today only."

"Yes sir."

"As of today only do you think you can take care of

the distribution & sale of 12 items of Poinciana Products?" He say.

I think about all the coolies on the street with no protection at all an I say. "I can handle 24 Mister Baron."

He slap his hand on the desk. All them ball points jump. "By GOD Lad I admire you spirit." He say. "Unless I a sadly mistaken judge of carrackter you gonna go far with the Poinciana Co."

Shitman I ressless to get movin. Have to deliver two sticks to Lu Ann. Then go out an push the ress of the stuff onta the coolies. An they is the bizness with Blood. Lot to do Man. No time aint got no time for this Royal Baron jazz.

He say. "But you unerstan how it is Son. This you first time out an they is a certain risk involved for me so I have to limit you to the 12 items. Matter of fack." He say. "Matter of fack it the policy of Poinciana to get a $10 deposit from the new Sales Men." He hold up his hand like I was gonna say somethin. I wasnt gonna say anythin. "Dont tell me Lad." He say. "I know you a poor son of the people an dont have the 10. I gonna show the trust I have in you. You can have the 12 items without makin no deposit an I *know* you be back by 6 oclock tonight with the $9 which is the rightful share of Poinciana Co."

"Yes sir." I say. "I be back Mister Baron."

"I know you will Lad." He tell me. He give me a big smile. "An I always know where to find my staff members if I need to find them." He say.

He give me the stuff.

At the door he shake my hand. "Now you a member of the Poinciana family. Good luck to you Lad."

Selling the stuff

Lu Ann and me we don't talk money no more. We got an arrangement with the Poinciana merchandise an Lu Ann say. "You all right with me Man. You makin you contribution."

Evry day I go up to Royal Baron's place and I get my consignment. "You doin a fine job Lad." Royal Baron say. "Keep up the good work an I increase you consingment."

Shitman I dont care if he never increase. It hard enough gettin rid of the little I got. Seem like evrybody on the street all ready got him self a supplier. Else they dont want or they aint got the bread or some reason like that you know. I meet a few other suppliers finely an they all sayin the same thing. "The bisiness is off." They say.

Dick Christmas to give you an instance. Evry body

callen him Father. We was sittin one day at Ritzies Bar drinkin wine and Father say. "Man I been peddlen up an down these streets 20 year an I never see the compitition so keen. Keen. Keen is whut it is Man."

"You can say that again Father." The other fella say. I dont know his name he peddles the stuff too. "Its cause they got kids like this walkin the streets an cutten in where us old timers broke in the territory. Thats what it is."

"Got to make a livin." I tell him.

"Sure you do." Father say. "Sure you do." He say to the other fella. "They room enough for evry body Man. Compitition good for the bisiness. It spread the word. It spread the idea of the stuff. It get the notion across to a lot of people. A hell of lot of folks it just never crossed they mind the possibility of usin the smoke for pleasure. Folks dont refuse pleasure when it offered them so cheap. Trouble with you." Father say to the other fella. "Trouble with you is you cant see pass you nose."

Other fella laugh.

Father say. "No I serious Man. In this bisiness you gotta take a look at the future an not just keep on thinkin about today an today only. I been a salesman 20 year off an on & I know whut I talken about."

"Off & on is right Man." Other fella say an he laugh.

Father say. "Man I hope that laugh is roofull an not one of pure an un adulterated glee."

"It aint pure an un adulterated." The fella say.

"Because it true I have learned my lesson an paid for it." Father say. "Yes I have learn an pay several time over."

"It true you bin a little un lucky." Fella say.

Father laugh an say. "Oh a little Man a little but I bin lucky now for a straight 3 year an I inten stayin that way."

"You not as young as you was once." Fella say. "An—"

"Now aint that a big fat discovry." Father say.

"Now dont get mad at me Father. All I mean—"

"Can out sell any 10 men on the street if I wanted to." Father say. "But I aint no money grubben hog like some who clutterin up the trade. I be a rich man today livin re tired on the Hill except I had the scroopels."

"I know you did." Fella say. "We all know you got them."

"Well then." Father say. He leanin across the table an an glarin at this fella.

69

"I know it." Fella say.

"Never did I knowingly sell to any youth under the age of 16." Father say. "Nor have I ever traded in habit formin forms of merchandise. I have run a clean shop for 20 years."

Fella say. "We all know it Father."

"An I got my luck back an I aim to spend the remainin years GOD has preserve for me on the outside."

"I with you on that." The fella say an he finish his wine an say so long. Father Christmas watch him go an he shakin his head all the time. "That fella." He say to me. "That fella who was just here?"

I say. "I see him Father."

"That fella is the kind of man I dont like. He take the ordinary business of buyin an sellin an give a criminal taint to it. You followin me?"

I say yes. He say. "That man could be on the corner sellin 5 cent news papers for 5 cent an he look suspicious doin it. Man the important thing the only thing is to survive. That the only problem we got in this world of ourn here on earth."

"That the truth Man." I say.

Father motion to Ritzie an she come over an take his glass an bring him back a fresh one. I like to watch her move. She see me an give me a big smile. "Now dont you stay too long Duke." She say an look out the winda.

Father sip his wine. He say. "Survivin is one thing but all the survivin in the world wont do you no good if you have to fool youself to do it. You follow me?"

I say yes I follow him but I have to get movin. An I leave Ritzies then given her a look when I go out pass the bar. She smile at me but I see it dont mean any thing.

Father Christmas crazy evry body know it. He always sayin. "You follow me?" An evry body say Yes but no body followin him. He been inside too much. Some who bin inside a lot get that way an they end up livin in rooms by they self with maybe a dog or a bird. Father live that way. Some people buy from him because of charity. Some of the people I took merchandice to they tell me. "Man Id like to give you some bisness but as long as Father stays outside I got to give it to him poor old man."

So I got the 12 a day to get rid of which is actually 8 or 9 because I keep out a couple or three for Lu Ann an me dependin on how I feel. An it never easy never an easy thing you know gettin the money out of the coolies because most of the time they dont have any. If they got it I can get it an I get it evry time. But it aint easy.

71

First you got to find them. After the first day they aint so easy to find Man I want to tell you that. Once they know whut you want they aint hangin out in the same places where they use to hang out an you have to go lookin for them.

The first day it was easy. They dint know whut I was promotin. I jus walk up to one of them coolies with a big smile an put it to him. They nothin they could do about it. Bein coolies they got no protection you know. They jus dont belong. They dont swing with the gangs an so they all alone. They say. "I neutral Man." An you say. "OK Man you neutral." An then you give it to them good they cant stop you. Cant stop nothing because they all alone in the world. Some time I feel sorry for them. I mean you know I feel sorry because they people an they dont have a chance.

Some of them dont have the money. I make sure they dont have the money an then I tell them I be aroun tomorrow an the next day an the nex an they better start havin the money. Some have the money but they dont like to give it up. They say. "Man I never touch that stuff. I in trainin Duke." They say.

I just give them my big fake smile. My big fake smile scare them bad because they know I dont mean that smile an they know who I am an whut I got behin me.

I say. "Buddy I dont care if you touch or not touch it. Give it to you Mother."

"My Mother dont use it Man." One of them tell me. I jus laugh at him an reach in my pocket. He say. "But I got a friend who touches it." He got the idee. Some of them so scared I mean the ones whut bought the stuff are so scared they probly jus thru it away. I dont care whut they do with it once they got it. Some coolies try real hard to hold out on me an then I have to push them to the wall. I jus slam them up hard against the wall an then I take out my blade an flip it aroun an let them see it you know an then finely they say. "Man dont you know I was only kidden?"

"Sure I knowed it." Is whut I always say an I give them that smile & I take they money & walk. I guess some of them use the stuff. An they was one I heard about. The word got back to me never mind how. One I heard about he was tryn to sell whut I had sold him to get his money back. So I had to go an have a talk with him an he stopped it. They see how things are if you talk to them straight. I mean they not dumb the coolies they just scared.

Most of the time I go up to Lu Ann in the morning. This is how I usually run my day. First thing you know I go to Royal an pick up the supplies. Then I make a few sales jus where I can. Any coolie I see on the street on the way from Royal to Lu Ann place I jus stop him an make a sale if he got the bread. Then I go up to Lu Ann.

Some days I kinda bisy or I dont feel jus like it or I meet some of the gang an so I dont get up to Lu Ann till late at night. She know if I dont come with the stuff in the morning why then I be there with it in the night. She know enough now to wait for me in Little Mans bed in the front.

I go in an some times Little Man layin on his fathers big bed an he still awake an I talk to him a while. Little Man he gettin smaller and smaller evry day it seem. Because now with his father gone and his brother gone he dont eat so good and he dont eat regular at all. Some times Savage or Bebop or Saint or one of the guys they remember to bring him some food but most of the time Little Man livin on wine. Drinkin from the muskatel we keep in the kitchen.

This night I went up he layin across the bed readin a comic book. "Duke Man." He say. Givein me a big smile. "Duke Man you got a smoke for me?"

I sit down on the bed an I tell him. "Little Man

this stuff costs me. I aint in the bisness for the fun."

"Listen Duke I give you 5 comic books for one smoke."

"Oh Man." I say.

"Half a smoke." He say.

So I give him half a smoke an he light up right away an pull in the smoke like he got a 30 day thirst an jus foun water. "EEEeeeyuh!" He say. "Thats good stuff Duke. Lissen Duke when we gonna burn on the Wolves? Aint we a fightin gang any more."

"You better talk to Blood about that." I say.

"I hear the Wolves aint fightin anymore." He say. "They all on junk an they give up fightin."

"Well if they aint fightin then we cant go down on them." I tell him.

"I dont care whether they fightin or not." He say. "We just walk into they turf an any Wolf we see we start boppin."

Little Man sittin there on the bed just wearin a shirt an the comic books scattered all around him. He startin to to work him self up. He start sayin whut he gonna do to the Wolves. "You talk to Blood about it." I tell him.

"I gonna talk to him Duke. I gonna talk to him."

I pick up the comic books an say to Little Man. "You better go to sleep now Little Man. You gonna need all the sleep you can get if you goin boppin."

"You right Duke." He say. An he close his eyes right away like he followin orders you know.

I blow out the candle an walk up front to Lu Ann. Dark in that room. She dont have the candel lit. I stop at the door an let my eyes try to see in the dark. Then I make her out on the bed and can see her skin an teeth shine in the little light from the windas. "Hi Duke." She say an she light a match and light the candel on the table. Glass of water by the candle.

"You have a rough day Duke?" She ask me. "Take off you shoes an come sit here beside me."

I sit down on the bed an take off my shoes. Then I take off my pants an shirt to be comfortable an we lay on the bed an read the comic books. She say. "That Little Man he lay aroun all day readin these books an wont never let me have one." So she read the one about the monster an askin me to tell her whut is this word and whut is that word. Some of them I knew an some I dont know. I read the Mighty Mouse. But they was only one Mighty Mouse book an when I finish it I dint feel like readen any more.

I reach into my shirt pocket an take out the 2 and a half sticks. Lu Ann put down her book about the monster an reach for them. "Duke Man you the deliverin angel." She say. She look at the half a smoke an say. "You bin smokin with out me?" I tell her I give it to Little Man for the comic books.

She twisted the end of the half a smoke so that none of the tobacco would fall out. Then she lit it on the candle an took a couple deep drags on it an handed it to me. "Little Man gettin crazier evry day." She say.

"He talken to me about burnin the Wolves." I say.

"Thats all he ever talken about." She say. "He aint right in the head any more." I handed her the butt an she finished it and put it out. We smoke it down till they only a little bitty piece of paper an tobaco left. Lu Ann roll it around between her fingers an make a little pill out of it. Then she take a regular cigarette out of her pack an pull some of the tobaco out of it. Then she put the pill in an we light up an smoke up the pill.

Lu Ann look at me an laugh. She laugh an laugh. "Whuts the matter with you?" I ask her.

"How come you stayin so far away from me Duke?" She laugh some more an I dont pay any atention because I know whut it is. Lu Ann dont need much to set her off. She say. "I know you in the same bed with me so how come you so far away Duke?" She laugh some more but she dont forget any thing. She remember to drink some water an then she hand me the glass. Drinkin water make the smoke go farther.

77

Then she lit up the second one. Evry time she in-hale a mouthful she close her mouth an put her hand on her chest an close her eyes. An she get this simple look on her face. It dont do all that for me. I mean it make me feel good but it aint so special about it like some people say. Like they say Man it tea for me evry time. But they just talk it into themselves. I mean its real mild. Some times it make evry thing seem far away an evry thing seem funny so you want to laugh at nothin at all.

We smoke the second one. Lu An say. "Oh honey I got eyes ony for you. Oh honey I burnin for you." She hand me the smoke an not takein her eyes off me like she gonna pin me to the wall with them. I take a deep drag an she put her mouth on mine an we drag together. Then she say. "Ah Duke. Ah Duke." I blow out the candle. She layin there with a big smile on her face. I put the smoke in her mouth an say. "Lasts." An she take a last big pull on it. "Put it out careful." She say. "That my breakfast you got."

She put her arms up to me and I come down to her. "Now lissen." I say to her.

"Ah Duke honey." She say. "Oh Duke sweet heart."

"Shut up Lu Ann. Shut up. Keep you mouth shut this one time. Hear?" I tell her.

She look at me. "I hear." She say.

Then when my eyes get uset to the dark again an I can see her face I see her mouth all stretched out tight across her face like she lockt it up. "No talk." I say to her. "Lu Ann. No sounds. No talk." An she just look at me with her eyes. An when she ready why her mouth opened an her face got all twisty but she dint make a sound an she dint say no words.

I stayed there with her beside her for a while then I got up and got dress in the dark. I walk down the hall an see Little Man sleepin spread out all over the bed. I see the light in the kitchen an I say to my self. "Duke did you leave a candle on in the kitchen?" But I knew I dint leave no candle on in the kitchen.

So I walked to the kitchen door real quiet. It was Blood there an he cleanin out the money box. His head down over the money box an I see ony the top of his head. He stuff the money in his pocket an when he go to blow out the candle I see his right eye. His right eye it was. Bulgin out an like hangin down on his cheek the way junkies do. He stand up an push back his chair not tryin to be quiet. Like he dont care who know it. Then he say. "I see you stanen there Duke. You jus keep on stanen there Duke cause if you make one move I kill you." Then he walked out an I let him walk. I just stan there an I can hardly breath because I knew hed a kill me. I hear it in his voice.

The time I got lost

Whut I remember is I remember the red dust an how hot it get from the sun on it. An I uset to go bare foot and the dust would ooze up between my bare toes like mud. That whut I remember earliest when my Mother lef me down home with Gramma Custis & I was 3-4 year old I guess.

They uset to get up real early in the morning down there like 5 oclock an we eat breakfast with Grampa Custis before he go down the road to work for Mister John Snipe. Or Snead or Snade. Somethin like that. Snead I think it was. He a farmer and Grampa Custis work the farm for him. On Sundays Grampa Custis get all dress up in a black suit an we all go walkin to that beat up church where he preach. After my mother come an got me and brought me up North they kill

Grampa Custis. That when Grama came up to live with us in Harlem.

I uset to sit in that church an they all singin an Grampa up on the pulpit. I always sit lookin up at the roof all fulla holes and cracks waitin for GOD to come. Evry Sunday Grampa begin his sermon the same way. He lift up both his arms an he say. "They crush thy people O LORD an say the LORD will not see."

"He see all right." Some woman say. Same woman evry Sunday. She say. "He see allright Revrend Custis. Dont you worry yo head."

Then these other women start cryin and sayin. "He see. He see. He gonna take care of us."

Grama Custis say. "He love us. He see whut happenin."

Grampa an old man an when they beat him up he got kill. So then Gramma came to live with us.

"You my only child anymore." She uset to say to me when I get outa my bed in the morning early and come to the table to eat with Grampa. She give me a hug an she say. "You my only child anymore. All the rest growed up and lef me goin north an south an GOD know where with some of them. For some of them dont so much as write to let me know they where abouts or the state of they health."

"Dont you worry." Grampa say. "We all gonna be together someday in his place."

"That true enough." Gramma say. "But I do wish to GOD they take the time to write me a line now an again." She squeeze me in her arms. "This chile here is the best of them all. He a sweet good baby."

"He a fine boy." Grampa say. "Take care you dont strangulate him with all that huggin."

"They keep on tearin us apart from one an other." Gramma say. "It seem they never stop."

Grampa say. "Things is gettin better all a time Mamie dont you cry dont you take on so in front of the child."

She holden me so tight I cant hardly breathe. Grampa standin at the door in his beat up overhauls. "I goin now." He say.

Sometimes we have an egg on the grits an after I thru eatin I uset to go out to the side of the road an watch the 7-8 year old kids walken to school. Some of them wearen shoes. One day I follow behin them to the school house. Half the windows broken an I can hear them singin My Country Tisuv Thee. Then I walk back home thru the woods cause I afraid of meetin Mister Snead an his dogs an I got lost. I got lost in the ferny woods wanderin aroun an finely I just set down near a little pond an just wait till they come

82

for me. I remember how hungry I was. I just set there on a log an waited an sang church songs.

Grampa finely found me. He laugh when he see me sittin there. He say. "Boy you got the most worryin Grama in Snade County. Praise GOD I foun you for if not I never go home again to Mamie." Then he pick me up an carry me out of the woods to the road. I guess I was maybe a block from the road all the time.

Goin down the road Grampa singen a song about the LORD and I can hear it vibratin in his chest an his heart goin boom boom boom. I remember how I tried to match my breathin to his breathin because I wanted to be just like him in evry way. I uset to say to myself. "When you grow up Richard you gonna be the biggest strongest man in the County like Grampa Custis." Once when he drive the wagon into town for Mister Snead he took me with him up on the high seat and Man it was like flyin. You know it was like I floated in the air all the way to town next to Grampa.

He tippen his hat to all the white men an sayin. "How you Mister Snipe. How you Mister Snout. How you Mister Snups." How you Mister Snip an Snap an Snut an all those names like that you know. They all smile at him an say like "Hows the preachin goin Revrent?" an like that. Same people that kill him after I leave to come up North with my Mother.

One man say. "That you boy Revrent? He the spittin image of you. You doin all right for an old man. You niggers keep pumpin em out."

"Yessir. Thats right." Grampa say. "Yessir."

That time he foun me lost in the woods he carry me home an when Gramma seen us comin she come runnin down the road to us. Cryin. An took me an carry me the rest of the way.

Finely I go to the park

The reason summer time such a gas an a fake is because it come on like it gonna last for ever but you know it aint. You think Man it slow. It goin slow. An then befor you know it it over. I dont let it fool me. I know I gotta keep movin.

I fast an I want time to go fast. Some times I standen on a corner an I get so itchy with the slow way time moving that I start to bang on the bus stop sign.

Evry time I think of that piece up in Priests draw I start to itch all over an I tell my self. "Man you got to get it. Then you get Blood removed an you be the biggest man on the street."

An then I see my self walken down the street an evry body know who I am. Duke Custis. President of the Royal Crocadiles. Gang get to be so big an strong the Youth people have to send us a Street Worker like the other fightin gangs have. Then you got reconition. Then you really part of the thing.

So finely I went to the Park with Rod because that the only way I could figure it you know. The money I making from Royal Baron I jus spendin it. Not makin enough to save any of it. Make 2-3 dollar a day. Man it just spendin money when whut I need is big coin so I can put some away for buyin the Colt. Shitman I can feel it heavy in my belt. I can see it blazin away on a dark street an Wolves droppin an I can smell the powder.

I can smell that cold smell in my nose like the smell of flashbulbs that time Mister Johnson jumped out the winda down the airshaft. An all those news paper fotografers was flashin away takin picktchers of his body an the smell come up the air shaft like gun powder.

But the way things goin I will never get that piece an I can see it rustin away in Priests draw with the animals head on it.

An then half whut I makin I give it right back to Baron for stuff for Lu Ann. She cant never get enough of it. An then you know most the time I just dont care. I mean I know I aint never gone to make it. You get to a time after you been tryen to make it an then you jus dont care any more. You say to you self. What the hell Man. An then you jus drift along like throwen you self in the east river an lettin the water jus take you.

So I figure it they jus 2 things I can do to raise the sum. One I can go down town an try to get the money from Chester. Or two I can go to the Park with Rod an see if I can pick up the 5 or 10 like he does.

Once maybe a year ago I went to see Chester where he livin with this guy an they said I had to go up the freight elevator. He lives with this man in one of those big bildings on the East Side in the 70s. I said. "Man I no delivery boy. I come here to visit a friend." This guy in a uniform standin at the door. He say. "Thats all right fella. You just take up the freight elevator like a good boy."

So I didnt go up. Chester would lend me the sum anytime. Chester my best friend we friends since we was little kids. I say to Chester. "Ches man I need me some bread." He just reach in his pocket and give it to me. Chester that way. Old Ches he met this man in the Park an this man tooken him home with him an Ches still there. White man. A good deal for Ches. First home he ever has.

Walked to the Park with Rod. Walked along the street thinkin of all the pennies I spent all these years an how if I hadnt a spent them an if I had saved them why then you know Id have enough right now for the Colt. But when you a kid you dont think about things like one day you gone to need a Colt you just spend the penny when you get it. I walked to the Park thinkin of all those pennies I got from my mother and her husbands.

I must a spent about a million pennies since I was five years old. Lickriss drops an wax bottles with sweet water in them. Broken up pieces of chocolate & gum drops & sour balls & jaw breakers that change they color. Chances on the penny punch board an I never won the bicycle or the horse they given away. It make me mad when I think of all those pennies I spent and now nothin to show for it. Blew it all on candy an when I have to buy the Colt I dont have the sum I need.

Rod say. "Now Man when we get there you just act like you been there befor."

I ask him whut I have to do an he say. "You know whut you have to do."

I say. "I don't know Man." Meanin that I do know but I dont know if I want to do it.

"Nothin to it Duke." He say. An then he tell me about it you know whut they like an how easy it is to pick up 5-10 dollar for one nights work. An I say.

"I dont know Man." I dont like the feel of it you know. I mean Man its all right to buy it but I dont like sellin it.

An all the time I thinken about the pennies I spent. For all that crap. An now when the time come I need a piece so bad I dont have the sum. My throat get all dry at the thought of that piece layen up there in Priests draw all black an oiled and just waiten to GO. My hand itchin for it. A piece is the key. Man its the screw driver. You got youself a piece why then evrything open up for you.

Finely we get to this certain place in the Park. It one of those play grounds with a iron fence aroun it in a circle an inside the circle is a sliding bord an swings an like that you know. In the day time those places full of kids an they Mothers. But at night the guys come.

Man at night Central Park a No Mans Land. Even the headbreakers stay out of Central Park at night. The Park go right down the middle of the City but Man that Park is all by itself. The City dont know that Park at night.

Around this play ground they a couple street lights but mostly they just light up the leaves on the trees. Makes the leaves get all shiny you know not like leaves in the day time. An all these guys standin around or

89

sitten on the benches where the Mothers sit in the day. Most of them wearen bermuda shorts these short pants that come down to the knees an long sox.

You can hear the cars an buses goin up and down Fifth Avenue but you cant see nothin of the street. That place like a club house an cut off from evry thing. Also they got these guys you know with the blue jeans an the leather jackets. They wearen they hair long an always komen it. They wearen boots an always loungen aroun like cow boys with they bellies stickin out. They look at us at Rod an me when we walk in an then they dont pay no more atention to us because they know we aint customers an customers is what they looken for.

This guy sittin on a bench he waves to Rod. Got a little white soft hand he waves. Wearen those shorts an a fancy belt with a shiny buckle of brass or some-thin like that you know. An we walk over to him. He say. "Rod Honey where you been keepen you-self? I was afraid you given us up. Whose you friend dear?"

Rod say. "This here is Tommy." Tommy the name I tell him to use.

"Hello Tommy." This guy say and he put out his hand an I shake hands with him.

He say. "You a sweet one." An he look me up an

down you know like he gone to buy me shoes an all. "I havent seen you aroun befor have I honey?" He ask me an I say No. "I thought so." He say. "Id a remembered if I seen you aroun befor dear." An he smile at me to show me he like me.

We sit down on the bench with him and him an Rod start to talkin about wheres this one an that one. Rod say. "How about that little fat guy you know Harrison. Aint his name Harrison?" An this guy say to Rod. "Dont say aint dear. Harrison was arrested by the cops at one of those terrble 42 Street movie houses a few days ago."

"Thats bad." Rod say like he feelin sorry for the guy. For Harrison.

An this fella say. "It was boun to happen dear. It was boun to happen the way Little Harry come on any cop could spot him. Be he never so blind Rod dear."

"Shame." Rod say.

"Yes. Well." This fella say. "I warn him. Oh I warn him a 100 times. But he such a sweet soul he cant believe bad of any body even the cops. I told him. You go *outside* looken like that Harry love an you boun to be picked up."

"Uh uh uh." Rod say shaken his head.

"But out he went & picked up he was & I jus hopen

he find kindrid spirits in the jail." An then he sat back an folded his hans in his lap you know like a little boy.

While they was talken 2 of them guys in the blue jeans wearen boots started a fight. The one with dark hair kept knockin down the blond guy. Evry time the blonde guy got knock down his hair fall over his face and he fix it befor he get up. Then when he stand up the dark guy punch him an knock him down again. Hit him in the face evry time an the dark guy not sayin a word but jus standin there with his eyes all crazy an the blonde guy letten him punch. Not defenden himself or showen anthing on his face. Just lettin himself get hit an knocked down. Couple time he took a kome outa his pocket and komed his hair befor he stood up to be hit again.

This fella we was sittin with looked over an watched them. He say to us. "They just not trust worthy. I mean they can be the dearest of dears but you have to be awful careful with them because they just not trust worthy. I don know what it is with them."

Rod say. "They jus not trust worthy."

"Thats it." This fella say. "They so terribly beat Rod dear an they get worse an worse. I can remember when they was such good fun. But now I would not touch them with Kid Gloves not I I wouldnt. They just as libel to explode in you face as not. They so un stabel."

"Thats it." Rod say.

Then this fella turn to me an put his hand on on my leg. I could feel it warm thru. "My name is Tommy too." He say. "Do you believe in Fate dear?"

I say sure I believe in Fate. An he studyin me all the time. So then he say. "This you first time out isnt it honey?" An when I stop to think how I gone to answer him he squeal like some kind of animal an say. "I knew it. I knew it. Why you sweet thing I dint think they was any one like you left in this evil world."

Then the two tall fellas on the next bench both wearen bermuda shorts they come over to where we was sittin. They say. "Hello Tommy." They walk like they fallen asleep.

"Why dont you two just toddel along." Tommy say like he sick an tired of seein them.

So one of these tall fellas says to the other one. "Would you believe Little Tommy could be so mean?"

An the other one say. "It does open you eyes to his true nature dont it?"

"Wont you interduce us to you new little friend Tommy?" The first one say. "Hello Rod dear." He say. "Tommy got me so up set I forgettin my manners."

Tommy say. "Dont bring you problems to us Arthur." He dont even look at him when he talken. "Jus run along an find you own friends."

Arthur say. "Well. Id a never believe it if I had not heard it with my own ears."

"You maken me very angry Arthur." Tommy say.

Arthur an his friend start to walk away. Arthur say. "I shall never speak to him again. Never. Never. Never. An after all his talk of sharin. I have shared an shared an shared with him an this is the thanks I get." Then he turned aroun an say to Tommy. "Tommy you the most selfish man in the world."

Tommy say to me. "Dont listen to him dear. He sick with jealousy." Then he say. "Oh I dont know why I let my self get so up set."

"You shouldnt let you self get so up set." Rod say to him you know like he care a damn if Tommy get up set or not.

"I know I shouldnt Rod dear but there. That is the way I am. I wunder if you would mind if I took you friend Tommy here for a little walk."

"Why sure." Rod say. "You go ahead. Little walk is whut you need." An he wink at me. So I get up an go with Tommy. I dont know why. One of those times. Whut the hell. I went along. We walk for a while not talken. Tommy hummin to him self. Finely he say. "This here is the bridal path. You know where they ride the horses."

He put his arm aroun me an I let him. He lead me off the path. "Over here." He say in my ear. "Over here. I know a real private place no one ever find us."

Hardy Byrd the athaleet

Now that I in bisness I out on the street a lot tryn to get up the sum to buy the piece from Priest. The street is three blocks long. That the territory an the Royal Crocadiles control it. Mostly they nothin but people on the street an ony stores at the corners. Like a tailor store at one corner an a vegtable store where they got some bins of potatos an things like that. But the vegtable store a front for the numbers an the cops is always raidin it. But the vegtable man pays his way an he never closed more than a hour. One time he was payin off some plane clothes men for weeks an weeks befor he foun out they wasnt plane clothes men. They was jus some guys with a racket. Walk in. Say. "We plane clothes men. Pay off or we shut you up." So the vegtable man paid off to them an he dint find out till the cop on the beat tole him.

On an other corner is the big super market. People call it the Bank because that where all the money go. The second big place is Daddy Beatitudes Church. It uset to be a little department store but Daddy made it into a church. His congregation got so big he now have two floors an lives him self on the third floor.

Evry week he changen the signs on the second floor windas an I always stop to read them. This one week the signs say. "Daddy Beatitude offer $50,000,000 to the Preacher who can prove GOD sent him to preach." Next one say. "Daddy Beatitude was born in Jerusalem an not in Clipton, N. Carolina." Also. "As Noah was before the Flood so is Daddy Beatitude before the Fire. St. Mathews 24 Chapt. 32 Verse." And. "Dont miss the Fire Hose Baptism. A woman who had not walked in 16 years was healed in one of these Baptisms. Also many others." I read them for kicks. Only the women go to hear him. Daddy got a good thing goin for him self. He got a big white Caddy an even though he got his hair grown down to his shoulders he got plenty of women.

The street fulla rackets. Evry body on the street bisy survivin an doin this & that to get thru the week an get up the rent an the bread for the super market. They some women open up a bisness right in they house for reading fortunes. Put out a sign sayin.

"Spiritual Advice." An they in bisness. Over on Lexington Avenue some gypsies open a fortune bisness in a store but they aint doin so good. The gypsy women tell you what you dreams mean. They sit out front all day an one of them feedin her baby right out in front of evry body. She dont care. Gypsies dont give a damn for no body. Inside the store they got a lot of colored scarfs hangin an curtains an things an it look real good. In the store winda they got a head with like a map drawn on it showen the bumps an what they mean. Right there over you forhead that bump mean Character. An they sell books teachin how to read you dreams. They dont make much of a livin I can tell you that.

Also on the street we got a drug store. Doc he do a bisness in cundums an Kwik-Kill rat pellets an stuff like that but all them bottles of medcine settin on his shelves gettin dusty for years. In his winda he got a little statue wearen a belt you know aroun for a rupture an he got some signs tellin you about how important it is you ougt to keep Regular an like that. He sell a lot of medcine for sick stomach. They a lot of people on this street have Stomach Trouble.

Mostly the street jus apartment houses an stoops. Long rows facin each other an no space in between excep one place where the bilding fell down. We had a club house in the ruin for a while but the City come an took away the ruin. It jus full up with junk that place now.

Mostly the street jus a dirty place. The bildings is dirty like they bin washt in dirt. It run down they faces. You sit on a stoop an look acrost the street at a house for a while an after a while it look like that house is cryen. Doc Levine ast me once. "Richard." He say. "I want you to describe for me the street where you lived." I tole him. "Just dirt." I say. But I dint know it then at the time I tellin you about. I dint know anythin else then.

I uset to walk that street like that street was all they was. I knew all the faces but I never mist any body when they went. They leavin the street to move to a projeck or move to Brooklyn or some wheres else. Then new people comin in an I get uset to seein they faces. Some that movin always. Take Saint. Saint in the Crocadiles. One year it was last year his family moved 16 time. Ended up in Brooklyn. Saint uset to take the subway ride for a 1 hour to be with the gang. Gang all he has. Then an other 1 hour back to Brooklyn. An he have to walk a long walk to the subway stop because he cant go through Wolves territory.

I dont know why they move aroun so much. Dont

get anywhere. Dont end up no better off. They jus move from one lousy apartment to an other lousy apartment. An they move from one lousy job to an other lousy job. They got a bad job in a laundry or a dry cleaning plant or the kitchen of a restarant they go an get an other job in the same kind of place. Saints father say. "Boy we cant move up but they cant stop us from movin horizontal."

People in an out of the street all the time. An at the end of the street loomin up is the projeck. Man when they tore down the bildings to make room for the projeck you could see all the crap them old bildings was made of. They just go whamo with the iron ball an a whole bilding come crashing down. Maybe ony the back wall standin an then you could see green walls pink walls all the colors people painted their walls.

Then they come with the steam shovels an start bilding the projeck an the whole thing start all over again. People paint they walls an fight the roaches an then it all start over again. Some time they goin to tare down the projeck because evry thing get taren down an it will be the same all over again.

Some times I think about goin to the gypsies an havin my fortune read. Some afternoons I go to the movies an see a double feature horror movie about monsters an things like that you know. One day nothin to do I said to my self why dont you walk over to Rikers Island an watch the baseball game.

So I walked over there. I went around the Wolves territory but I guess they heard I was aroun cause when I crossen Second Avenue two Wolves in a stolen car try to run me down. Car come out of no where slammin at me. I jumped to the side walk an whip aroun a light pole. People standen there with they mouths open watchin. I jus walk off like nothin happen. Cool you know.

I got to the east river an walked across the foot bridge. Guard look at me an say. "No trouble now. I remember you."

"First time I ever here." I tell him.

I walk pass the bilding where they keep the crazy people an out to the baseball diamond. Sit down on the grass an watch the game. Hardy Byrd playin first base an it a pleasure to watch him play.

Hardy a friend of mine from the street. He the only coolie I look out for. Hardy a big athaleet he plays football an baseball & basketball & all the track games. He in high school now an all the colleges after him with contracts. Hardy gonna make it big in the sports game. So he gotta keep himself clean an we help him out. Hardy could come in with the gang if he wanted to but he have a good thing goin in the sports.

Hardy is very fast an I like to watch him. He fast but never jerky. Moves like light that man I get nervous watchin him. You keep you eye on him evry minute he still move with out you seein him move. Moves like a hunter an he always is where the ball is.

After the game I walk back with him. He got his glove on his belt an he bouncin along on his sneakers like the athaleets do.

I ask him did he decide on a college yet? An he say yes he decided.

"I goin to one of the white ones." He say. "They offer the best deal." He say. "Well I tell you Duke I will play football for them an basketball an baseball. But no track. I aint gonna run my heart out for them."

The big night an how it all happen

In those apartments we all liven in the kitchen the big room. The whole family eat in the kitchen. They usely a big table for eatin on an most kitchen have a bed also because they need the room for sleepin. Up at Little Mans place the kitchen our club room. We sit aroun the table an talk an drink muscatel when we got it.

All the guys in the Crocadiles who are users now buyin they smokes from me. If they dont have sufficient bread to get into Lu Ann why they usely spend whut they have for a smoke. We sit aroun the table some of the guys smokin and some drinkin muscatel an we talk about things. Like how the Crocadiles was in the old days when we was a real fightin gang an uset to go down on the Wolves.

It always the new guys who do the most talken. The ones who never been with us when we went down on the Wolves in the old days. The Crocadiles now got a lot of young guys who been in the gang for a while but aint never took part in a street fight because we aint been fightin lately. They talk about the old fights like they been with us. Like you hear Bebop sayen. "An remember when Little Man ripped off the car aireal an slashed his way out breakin thru 12 Wolves." Bebop never even with us. He hear about it so many time he think he was with us. He wasnt with us.

I dont say nothin. I jus let them talk. The talk is good for them. It all start because of the Wolves tryin to run me down in the car the day I went to Rikers Island. All the guys want to revenge me. Three days now they sittin aroun sayin why dont we go down on them and lets burn them. They all waiten for Blood to come but he aint showed since the night he emptied the bread box.

Rod say. "He aint comin back. No use sittin aroun watin for him."

Saint say. "You right about that Man. Blood dont have the Crocadiles in his heart no more. All he thinkin about his junk an all he want is bread to buy H. He never comin back."

Savage say. "But he dint have our permission to resign. He jus cant walk out on the gang. Its in the rules Man."

"Junkies dont know Rules." Rod say. "Whut we gotta do is elect a new President." An he look at me. Evry body look at me. I dont say nothin. I take a sip of muscatel. Rod say. "Ony way we become a fightin gang again is we elect a fightin President. Some body with a lot of heart."

"I think he gonna come back." I say. "I think Blood gonna come back for an other look in the bread box. We aint seen the last of him."

"Maybe you right." Cowboy say. He standin in the door comin back from Lu Ann. Cowboy a cocksmith. Cowboy say. "An when he come back." An he make a move with his hand.

Rod say to him. "You gonna do it?" Rod dont like Cowboy because it was Cowboy who always uset to bring the girls in in the old days when we was a fightin gang. "Any thing got to be done." Rod say to Cowboy. "Anything got to be done we know where we can find you. You be inside pounding the hoar."

Cowboy look at him quiet like you know. Then he say. "It better than bein a hooker in Central Park." An befor Rod can say anything he say. "It better than bending for kicks an bread on a Park bench."

Rods eyes they get all narrow you know an he study Cowboy.

"None of that now." I tell them. But they dont hear me. When a mans blood rise he dont hear nothin but the blood an he dont see nothin but the man in front who soundin him.

Rod say. "You soundin me Cowboy?"

Cowboy give him that big smile whut aint a smile.

"Break it up." I warn them. An the guys putten down they glasses of muscatel an they comic books an slow movin out of the way. I jus sit there with my muscatel an watch Cowboy an Rod both. Especially Rod cause it up to him to make the move.

Rod put the challendge again. "You soundin me Cocksmith?" He say. "Big Pussy Man you soundin me?"

Cowboy smilin still that smile like it froze on his face. He say. "Lover Boy. . . ." An he never finish sayin whut he goin to say because Rod make his move risin to his feet an the blade open in his hand befor I see how it got there.

"Put that away Rod." I tell him. "Put it away." He dont listen. He movin slow tord Cowboy.

Cowboy still smilin. He dont reach for his blade yet. Cowboy playin it big an cool. "How come you aint wearen bermuda shorts yet Lover Boy?" He say.

An Rod make his first thrust. Cowboy take one step back movin smooth but he stop smilin now an reach for his blade. It go Thnick when he open it an Bebop settin there in a corner of the kitchen say "Uhh" like he got it in the belly. Bebop dont even know he said it.

They standin lookin at each other now an not movin except the blades movin in little circles. Candle lights shinin on the blades an on they sweaten faces. All you can hear is how they breathin. Cowboy wipe the sweat away from aroun his mouth with the back of his lef hand. Rod waitin for that. I knew it comin soons I saw Cowboys hand goin up to his face. That was his bad move. When the hand start to drop Rod make his cut an mark Cowboy from elbow to his wrist. Cowboys arm runnin blood. Droppin off his fingertips. He gonna need stitches I say to my self. I jus watchin now. I know it no good tryin to stop them now. When theys blood already they wont quit till they is more blood.

Cowboy shake the blood off his hand an put the smile on his face again. "Try that again." He say to Rod an Rod he make an other cut but Cowboy he step in side an slice Rod straight acrost the chest cuttin his shirt real neat. An the blood folla the cut in a straight line. Rod dont look down. Now he got like a apron of blood on his chest down to his belt.

Now it time I say to my self an while they both standin there breathin an watchin each other I move. With my right arm I knock down Rods knife arm an with my lef at the same time I push Cowboy flyin back against the wall. "All over." I tell them. "Thats it." I take a look at Cowboy an see he ready to quit so I can turn my back on him. He ready. He slum down on the floor an put his bad arm on his lap. I turn aroun then an hussle Rod to a chair. I dont give him time to say nothin. I say. "Man we gotta take care of that."

"Yeh." Rod say.

I start to take off Rods shirt an he jus sit there an let me do it. The cut a nice clean line acrost his chest an the blood comin regular. Savage lookin at Cowboys arm. Savage tell him to move it an to make a fist. "OK." Savage say. "It aint a serious cut. No tendons or mussels cut. We jus wrap it up good an you keep it quiet maybe you wont have to go to the emergency."

"I jus tell em I was slicin bread an the knife slipt." Cowboy say.

Savage say. "You can tell em but they wont believe you."

In the meantime I tellin Bebop to get the armory out an he go inta Little Mans room an pull the box out from under the bed. Box got our weapons in it an some banages an cotton an iodine we pick up here & there. I put a banage on Rods chest an draw it real tight windin it on thick a whole role of it. When I finish Rod light up a cigarette an pour him self a glass of muscatel. He roll up his shirt an throw it out the window. I tell Bebop to go get him a shirt an Bebop finds one belongin to Little Man an Rod put it on. Tight on him but it cover the banage.

Cowboy all fixed up. He carryin his arm gentle holdin it by his thum hooked in his shirt. He come over an get him self a glass of the wine an he say to Rod. "You a real man Rod. I sorry I sounded you."

"Thats all right." Rod say not lookin at Cowboy.

Evry body quiet then for a minute. Guys movin back to the table an pickin up they comic books an things where they lef them. Bebop say. "Any body know where is Little Man? He wasnt here when I came here an he still not here."

No body seen him.

"He all right." Somebody say. "He prolly out to see the All New Monster Show at the movies."

Some of the other guys come in then an we all sit aroun talkin and drinkin. One of the fellas who jus come in Bishop I think it was buys a smoke from me an Mau Mau went up front to Lu Ann. When he come back China got up an went in to her. I put Bishops dollar in my pocket an kep my hand on the bread. 8 dollars of it belongin to me of the 20 in my pocket.

I almos yelled out loud. Oh Man! 8 big bills an I on my way. I gettin there. An other 2 days an other big push with the smokes an I got it made. I dont even have to go back to Central Park with Rod. Oh Man! I can feel the piece in my hand. An other day an other 2 days an I have it in my hand. Then Man we a fightin gang again a boppin gang again we go down on the Wolves an we burn. 5 dollar from the Park an 3 dollars mine from the sale of Poinciana products.

I almos laugh out loud thinkin of Royal Baron that crazy west indys black English man. Tellin me I can have a car an a apartment of my own an friends of both sexes. Workin my ass off an still I dont have the price of a beat up old piece. But Man I makin it. I see it in my hand that piece all shiny with oil layin up there in Priests draw with the brass head on it. Rememberin how the draw go slump when he close it. Slump. An the door open the kitchen door an Blood standin there.

Blood jus stan there in the door an no body say a word. Blood laugh his crazy laugh an close the door.

He say. "Well I glad to see all you men here."

"How you doin Blood Man?" Some of the guys say.

"Cant complain Man." Blood say laughin. He high as a kite on the junk. Man he flyin. His head sorta wobblin on his neck an his right eye kinda hangin out you know. "Glad to see all you motherens here. I gonna whip this gang back into shape. I gonna whip it back inta shape uh uh uh Man this gang this gang gonna see some disiplin befor I get thru with it. Gang jus fallin apart. Uh uh comin apart at the seems you know Man. I gonna put it back to gether an we be the real Crocadiles again fightin an burnin on the Wolves an bein real men."

When junkies high they talk real big. A junkie walk up to you an say. "Man I gonna kill you." If he dont take a blade out or a piece right then an there why you got nothin to worry you. If he say. "Man you wait here 20 minutes an I kill you." Why you know he aint gonna do nothin because junkies dont know nothin about time an they gotta make they move right then an there or they dont make it. Like they forget all about it. While they lookin at you they movin into another world an you can be standin right in front of them then an they dont even see you. I mean they see you but they dont see you because they aint with you anymore.

I sat at the table an waited for it to happen with Blood. Knowin it was goin to happen. Watchin & waitin for it to happen. Because when it happen I goin to make my move. I say to my self watch for it Man.

One second he standin there at the door like the biggest man in the world. Like a general soundin his troops. "We gonna do some head breakin our selfs." He sayin. Then he walk over to the table an sit down. "Next week." He say. An I knew I had him. "Next week I gonna start puttin you back in shape again an then we gonna draw up plans an send out the snakes an get the armory fixed up."

"You aint gonna do nothin Blood." I say quiet like. Evry body look at me an then they look at Blood. Blood just sit there an he smile at me. "You my War Lord." He say to me smilin. "You my War Lord Duke Man."

"I aint you nothin Blood." I tell him.

"I thought you was my War Lord Duke." He say real sad like. "Aint you my War Lord Man?"

I jus look at him.

He say. "Well Duke Man if you aint my War Lord I want you to be my War Lord. I thought I made you War Lord long time ago Duke Man. You wanta be my War Lord Duke Man?"

I dont say any thing. I jus smile at him acrost the table. He pour him self a glass of wine an I reach over an take it away from him. He dont try to stop me. All the guys laugh at him. He scratch his face. He look aroun at evry body. "How you doin Saint Man?" He say. "How's the Man?" Saint dont answer him. Blood say. "Uh uh uh now I tell you startin next week we got some hard work ahead of us gettin back in shape again."

Then he look at me an wait to see if I gonna say any thing. He picks up those big hans of his an slams em down on the table all the glasses jump an the wine slosh. "You son ofa bitch Duke you motheren I gonna kill you with my bare hans." He puts his head back an yells from low down in his throat. "Ahhhhhhhh." We stan up at the same time an I feel my goddam heart pumpin an Rod hand me his blade.

Blood swayin on his feet an he got white spit in the corners of his mouth. He scream an evry body move back from the table. I move tord Blood keepin my left hand touchin the table. Followin it aroun till it lead to Blood. I get half the way to him. I raise my knife arm an Blood take one step back. An then they a knockin at the door.

Evry body stand still an they aint no sound. No sound at all. Knockin again. An then some body say.

"Open up. It me. Cherokee." Some body go an open the door.

I keep my eye on Blood an Blood keep his on me. Evry body else look over at Cherokee. I hear Cherokee say. "Shitman this aint no time for blades. Clear out of here. Clear out. Little Man dead on a 118 Street killed by the Wolves."

Evry body move fast to the door. Blood put up his knife and start to go. He say to me. "I come back an take care of you Duke."

"You aint never comin back Junkie." I tell him.

He say. "You son of a bitch Duke. You motheren. You see if I dont come back. I come back an I gonna kill you."

He leave then. An I say to the guys. "All right. Fade. An stay off the streets. The headbreakers will be thick out there tonight."

They all say. "You right Duke Man." An Rod say. "Things gonna be a lot diffrent aroun here now Duke in command."

"Rod the new War Lord." I say. "That OK with you guys?"

The guys say OK it all right with them. That how I get to be President.

After the big night

I locked the door an listened to they steps goin down the stairs. Then I put out the candles an walked in to the front room where Lu Ann layin on the bed smokin an lookin at a comic book. I blew out her candle an went an watched the street from the winda.

Lu Ann say. "Whut was goin on?"

I watchin the out side an I dont answer her.

She say. "I thought I hear Bloods voice. Whut was goin on all that noise an all that quiet I knew somethin goin on."

I lean out the winda a little ways an see the guys comin out one & two at a time an disapeerin on the street. One right after an other like they meltin right inta the side walk. They know that street Man. They know evry hole an corner. I see Blood walkin off by him self. No one with him. He stumble down the street. Headin for Ritzies prolly.

Lu Ann say. "Man you blockin whut air they is. Get away from that winda."

I wait till all my boys is out an away. Then I go over an stretch out on the bed. Lu Ann say. "Whut was goin on in there? Did I hear right thinkin it Bloods voice I hear?"

"You hear right." I say. I tell her whut happen. About Rod an Cowboy an Blood an me.

She say. "Blood really thru now."

"He thru all right." I say.

"You the big man now Duke." She say. She lean up on her elbow an look at me. "I knew it first time I saw you Duke you was gonna be the big man." She touch my mouth with her fingers an lookin at me. Then she put her hand under my shirt an touch my chest. "You want to make it with me now Duke?"

I dont answer. I dont feel like talkin. "Any thing you want Duke Honey?" She ask me.

I tell her Im tired an want to go to sleep.

"I will go to sleep too." She say.

But I cant sleep an jus lay there lookin at the ceelin where a square of light from the winda is. So tired I dont even take off my clothes. No wind comin in that winda even when no one in front of it. Lu Ann say. "Youd think a skinny girl like me woulden feel the heat so bad but I do."

I lay there an look at the light on the ceelin an I can hear people movin aroun up stairs on the floor above an I hear some cars pass on the street. Some one cryin below. A baby or a girl. An you can hear the cryin comin up the air shaft an voices not sayin anythin you can make out. I think about Little Man. In the cooler now. In the cold box. Waiten to be identifyd. Old Little Man. Thinkin about how Rod wearen his shirt now. Thinkin about how we gonna revenge them motheren Wolves for what they done to Little Man. Old Little Man no one ever goin to come identify. Finely they bury him some place.

"San Fran cis co." Lu Ann say. "I like that name." She say it again. "San Fran cis co. San Fran cis co." She raise up on her elbow again holdin her little face in her hand. "Duke you ever think about San Fran cis co? About ever goin there? Some times I think about it all the time." She say.

"You been there?" I ask her.

"No I never been there. But I seen it in the movies. It look so cool an clean Man you know. Some time I jus gonna take off for that place like a big bird."

"You gonna walk?"

117

"Buy a ticket on the Grey Hound for all the money I got. Go as far as I can go. Then work for a while an start out again. I know I could make it if I ever get started."

"Whut you gonna do when you get to San Francisco?"

"I will always find some thing." She say. Then she quiet for a while an the cryen in the air shaft stopped. "You know they got an ocean in San Fran cis co?" She say.

"I know it." I tell her.

She look at me. "Then whut ocean they got?"

"They got the Pacific ocean." I tell her.

"Now Duke how did you know that?"

"Jus know it."

She say. "You know whut Duke? I would go all that way jus to see the ocean? You know that?"

"You dont have to go all that way jus to see an ocean." I tell her but she aint listenin. She say. "I see pictures of the ocean but I jus cant believe it. How can it be like that Duke?"

"Just is." I tell her. "Lissen." I say. "Lu Ann. You dont have to go all that way to San Francisco to see the ocean. We got an ocean right here."

"Where we got an ocean right here?" She sit up she get all excited.

118

"Got an ocean out at Coney Island." I say. "You can get there on the subway."

"Get on the subway an it take me to the ocean? Duke you gassin me?"

"Truth Lu Ann."

"Lissen Duke." She say. "You take me out to the ocean first thing tomorra hear? I pay you way too."

"I take you Sunday. Cant go tomorra."

"That a promise Duke?" I tell her sure I take her Sunday. She say. "I never be able to sleep now knowin you have an ocean an I goin to see it Sunday."

"Where you from Lu Ann you dont know about the ocean out at Coney?"

She say. "Now Man you aint gassin me you really got an ocean you can get to on the subway?"

"You see it for you self Sunday."

Finely she went to sleep an when I woke up it was still dark but gettin light. I took off my close then an set by the winda and smoked a cigarette. They a little wind that time of night. Lu Ann layin on her side with her head on her hands like a baby. Where she from? I wonder. An whut will happen to her whut will become of her? When it get light I go inta the kitchen an make some coffee. Lu Ann got a pot an a can of coffee. When I go thru Little Mans old room I hold my breath an not look at any thing.

119

The lion

When I first come here to this place. When they
brought me to this place the doc Doctor Levine he
all the time askin me. "Richard tell me about the
dream you had last night." An he sayin. "You dont
seem to have any dreams at all Richard. But I know
you do. Well when you feel like talkin about you
dreams to me I be waiten Richard."

In this dream I haven all the time or you know
maybe two-three times a week since I was say 12 years
old in this dream they aint no people in the city. Or
they *is* people but its like you cant see any of them
because they all in the houses. I told Doctor Levine
when I finely told him about the lion that it aint easy
to tell about. You know like when the doctor say.
"Now show me where the pain is." An you try to

point to it but when you point to it you cant be sure anymore thats where it is.

I never give any special atention to the lions at the Zoo. I mean like they aint my favorite animal or anything like that. I walk by the lion cage I look at the lion. Thats all. Same way I look at the seels or the elephants. Any way I dont go there more than 1 or 2 time a year an I dont have a favarite anamal.

Only one time any thing special happen was the time I was passen the lions cage. He jus layin there with his big yellow eyes not lookin at anything. An then way far away they was an explosion. Boom it went. You couldnt hardly hear it like maybe it was over in Jersey or somewhere. All the people at the Zoo they jus kep on walken aroun. But I hear it. And the lion he hear it. He lift up his big old head an he growl. Not loud. Jus quiet like way down in his throat. You know.

See in this dream it always start out the same way. Aint nobody on the streets. Like it was three four oclock in the mornin. Ony it has to be later than that because the sky is yellow. I never see the real sky colored yellow like this one. But it yellow all right like a lemon.

Then the wind start blowin. It dont make any noise but you know it a wind because things start blowin aroun you know. Like the news stand on the corner gets blowed over an all the papers blow away. An all the crap on the streets start blowen. An the signs. The signs that say PLAY STREET DO NOT ENTER an NO PARKIN an BUS STOP. Evrything that aint nailed down start flyin an rollin down the streets not maken any noise.

The sky turn green then. Not dark you know but like the inside of a lime. An the East River is all black and shiny like it a river of oil. Or like coal. An the big neon signs fall down an break an crash with out no sound. The super market sign that say BUYWELL SUPER MARKET and the liquor store one. All get blown down an the wind blowin dust evry old which way dust comin out of the cracks in bildings.

I see myself layin on the couch all scrunched up waitin. My toes all curled up an I waiten. Because I know whut comin. The lion.

It come. It there. You dont see it way off it you know way off comin closer an closer but you see it all of a sudden. It jus there. All over the sky. An like he aint flyin. You know he just like sittin an not movin. But he movin all right. But he dont really move you know. Like he stay put an the city come to him. He spread out across the sky an his skin the color of sand. He come in over Washington Heights and he dont hardly touch it an it fall down. The George Washington Bridge. Falls down in the river. Then he heads down town an the bildings fall they go crashin down knockin into each other. Whole city fallen down under him. He jus touch it an it go. It jus fall apart an go crashin down. It come to pieces an the dust fillen the sky. Where the lion was the sky all black an he keep movin into where the sky is clear. He open his mouth. Christman he open his mouth and bite the Crysler Bilding in half an the Empire state an all them sky scrapers. Chomp. An they gone. Chomp.

Man. Aint nothin left when he get thru. The whole city jus one big beat up pile of crap when he get thru with it. I layin there on the sofa an I watch it go. He go Chomp an it all fall down in ruin the whole city.

A busy day

When I finish drinkin my coffee I lock the door behin me an start out on the day. Got a lot of things to do an take care of.

Early an no body on the street yet except Mister Hurst carryin in the empty garbage cans with his pipe dead in his mouth. "You up bright & early." He say to me. "Or aint you been to sleep yet?" That man Mister Hurst he got a voice even when he talken soft it go boomin back an forth between the bildings. Bouncin from one side the street to the other like a billard ball. He take the pipe outa his mouth an say. "You mother lookin for you last night."

I keep movin. "You tell her you see me." I said.

"I hear a friend of yours got him self killed last night." He say.

"Little Man."

"I hear it was a boy name Arthur Davis."

"That the name his parents give him." I tell Mister Hurst. An he say. "Now I suppose you an you friends gonna go down on the Wolves an revenge Arthur an get a few more of you killed. When you gonna stop it Duke?"

"I dont know whut we gonna do." I say.

"The Wolves know. They know and they waitin. When you gonna stop this crazyness Duke? You lettin the world push you into crazyness Boy. You no bettern a junkie when you let them push you down so far."

"No body push me aroun." I tell him. "No body."

"Boy." He say. "You gettin the worst pushin of all."

"I no diffrent than any body else." I say.

"I know that." He say. An he bend down an with one hand pick up three cans piled on top of the other. I smile to my self thinkin about him bein carryed down 5th Avenue in my dream. King of the Negroes. King of the Garbage Cans that whut he king of.

"I dont know whut the world got to do with it." I tell him. "The world aint such a nice place."

"They be goin to the moon soon." He say. "You can try that. May be it be better for you." He carry the cans in side an he dont look back at me.

125

Hurst live in a cellar an dont know whut the world all about. He dont know the world run by crooks pushers an hood from the top to the bottom. In the White Houses an in the vegtable stores on the corners all of them got big hands in the pie. Its no world to be nice in. If you want the littleest crumb from the pie you got to fight you way to it. Evry body runnin an screamin for they little bit. Once you get you hand in the pie Man you got it made. Whut Mister Hurst got? He got a room that keep him warm in the cold that whut he got.

I dont want none of that. I rather be dead like Little Man than work my life out haulin garbage cans or breathin steam in a laundry in the Bronx like my Mother. We dyin all the time but when you get you hand in the pie you live to be old like them white hair women on Park Avenue they walk with canes but they still alive. Unless some body cut you down while he tryen to get his. Well Man that the chance you take. You dont want to take the chance why you live in the cellar. Carry the garbage cans an fight the rats till you dead.

Walkin tord Lexington that morning early was the first time I thought about it at all. Talkin to Mister Hurst an Little Man dead on the street was whut made me think about it at all. But thinkin about it dont make do diffrence because whut diffrence can it make? I mean Man you do whut you do with out ever thinkin about it an then you think about it an you keep on doin whut you been doing. Dont make no diffrence. You jus do whut you do.

Walked to Lexington an turned uptown walkin to Priests. Stopped at the gypsy store an looked at the head in the winda all mapped out. Love bump is over the left ear. The gypsy woman whut feeds her baby out where evry body can see it standin there now in the open door eatin a orange. She say. "How about it Boy? Be my first customer today I give it to you for a dollar even."

"Got no time now." I tell her.

"Now the time." She say. "Now the time Boy. Dont be puttin it off. I can see lookin at you this an important day in you life."

I look at her eyes. How she know that?

"Fifty cents Boy. What you say Boy? 50 cents an I put all my mysterical power at you command. Come in Boy an it be the best 50 cent you ever spend."

So what the hell I thought an I went in. She got a glass ball at a table an two chairs. I sit down acrost from her. She say. "Now how you want it? You can have it from the cristal ball here it never lie. Or the cards. Cards is always good. Or I read you bumps.

Which ever way you want Boy. I dont believe in palms." She say. "Some gypsies cheat you with the palms but not me. White man come in here yesterday an want me to do it to his palms. I tell him get outa here I dont do it to palms. Some gypsies cheat you." She say. "How you want it Boy?"

"I like that cristle ball." I tell her.

She put her hand on it. "It never lie." She say closin her eyes.

"But I like the cards too." I say.

"You my first customer today Boy. For good luck I give you some of the ball an a little of the cards. How you like that Boy?"

"That OK."

"How much money you got Boy?"

"Got 50 cents." I tell her. "You said 50 cents. That all I got."

"OK Boy. I do it for you for 50 cents."

She push back her long black hair an hold her hands along side her ears holdin her hair back. She lean for ward I can see her tits but she dont care she all ready showed them to the whole street feedin her baby.

"I see you been thru some trouble lately Boy. But now you comin out of it an the road ahead is clear. For a while any way it clear. Then they be trouble again. Ball gettin all cloudy now." She look at me. "How old are you Boy?"

I tell her I 18. She look at me an she say. "Ball tell me you a 14 year old." I dont say nothin. Theys some thing to it you know when they can figger out how old some body is. Evry body believe me when I say I 18 except my Mother an Gramma Custis. Evry body. But that cristle ball knew other wise.

"I look at the cards for you now. I givin you you money worth Boy." She shuffle the cards. "No body ever come in here get so much for 50 cents." She spread out the cards in a circle an bent over again pushin her hair back. "Looka that." She say tappin the Queen of Diamonds. "You know whut that mean?" She shake her head. "I givin you the Truth Boy. Means a blond woman gonna be the bearer of bad news." She look up an catch me lookin at her tits. She say. "Right next to it the Ace of Clubs. That aint the death card you jus mist the death card. But that card mean you gonna be close to some one dead."

"Friend of mine got killed yestaday." I said. "That mus be him." I lookin down at the card now.

She say no. She say it like this. "Nah nah nah Boy. I tellin you about the Future. Any body can tell you about yestaday. It the Future when you gonna be near some body dead."

I try to figger out who it could be. She put her hand acrost the table palm up. "50 cents." She say. I give her the 50 an she pull up her big skirt an stick it inside some where.

"That all you gonna tell me?" I ask her.

She say. "Boy that all I see. I tell you all I see. You want me to make up lies an cheat you like other gypsies? I tell you the Truth an if I dont see it I dont tell you."

I say OK an leave her place. I can smell the cookin in the back room where she keep her baby. When I go out the door she say. "You watch out for that blond woman because I dont like the looks of her."

I walk on down the street an I feeling hungry so when I come to Hermits I decide may be I go in have a sandwich. He still got the pictures of Nkruma an Nasser in his winda. I go in an sit down at the counter. Some coolies get up an leave. Hermit say. "Now I dont want any sellin in here."

I jus rock on my stool an give him a smile.

"Ruinin the Race with the products of white civilization." He say. He throw up his hans. "Whut do you know about it. Damn it Man you ever hear of Benin?"

"He the pusher over at a 118 street?" I say.

Hermit look at me like I make him sick.

I say. "I want a ham sandwich an a coke."

He dont even hear me. "Benin a place in Africa where a high civilization a high *black* civilization flourishin when europe runnin with savages. An Mahomey." He say. He drop his hans an look out the winda. "Oh Man when I thinka Mahomey." Then he make me the ham sanwich finely. He stan there watchin me then he sit with one leg on the sink an say. "Got a letta from Monrobia yestaday."

"I hope it good news." I say.

"You know where Monrobia is?" He ask me.

"Sure I know." I tell him.

He say. "Monrobia is the capital of Liberia an Liberia in AFRICA."

"I know it. How bout fixin me that coke Hermit?"

He make the coke. Put it in front of me an say. "They a Mister Hardison in Monrobia a big man in the government offerin me a partner ship in a lumber company. 500 dollas."

"You got the money Hermit. Sell out an go."

"I thinkin of it." He say. "I givin serious thought to it."

"Lot of lumber in Africa Hermit. You likely become a million aire if you get it all chop down."

He say. "You a damn fool boy. A man want money he can make it here but AFRICA our real home an Liberia the place we can be free like no where else in the whole world."

"You feel that way about it Hermit that where you ought to go. What you hangin aroun here for?"

He shake his head. "Lord Man I dont know. Dont know why I jus dont pick up an go. It aint so easy when you my age to start a whole new life. If I was you age I woulden think twice. Id jus go I swear I would. When you live to be as old as me in this one place why then that place is home even if it aint really home an even if you aint free."

When I leave he say to me. "Give it some serious thought Duke. That the place for a young strong man to feel free an make some thing of him self. Stay aroun here an you end up like that kid they foun on the street las night."

"He a friend of mine." I tell him.

Hermit say. "Duke Man I know he a friend of yourn that why I talkin to you. I am not a man talk jus to hear the sound of my voice. When I tellin you about AFRICA an the movement I speakin from my heart Duke."

Then I walked up to Royal Barons place for my days supply. Royal cracked the door open like he does an let me in. "Well Lad it always a pleasure a real pleasure to see you." Miss Dewpont sittin they in a blue flimy thing you can almos see right thru. Royal Baron say. "I dont remember if I have the pleasure of intraducin you to my secetary Miss Dewpont."

Miss Dewpont say. "Why surely Roy Mister Baron. I met this young man on his first visit." An she give me her big smile an I say hello.

Roy put his han on my shoulder. "You doin a great job Lad." He say. "Bearen out all the faith I had in you." While he talken to me he slip the supply in my pocket. "You rapidly becomin one of the leaders of my entire Sales Orginization an I woulden be a bit surprise if you didnt one day soon rise to the very top an become Ace Number 1."

He go over to his big desk an pick up one of the Ball Point pens. He clip it on to my shirt pocket. "Id like you to have one of my own personal Ball Point pens Lad." He pat me on the shoulder again. He say. "Givin you that pen is part of my personell incentive plan." He look at Miss Dewpont.

"That a lovely idea Roy Mister Baron." She say.

When Baron open the door for me Miss Dewpont wave her hand to me. "Good luck Lad." She say.

So I walkin down the street then bouncin a little on my heels an wonder is the word out yet. Do the people seein me know I the President of the Royal Crocadiles? Lot a people see me they say. "Hiya Duke. How you?" Maybe they know. I go on up to the Club House.

Few of the guys sittin aroun the table. Lu Ann wearin one of Little Mans shirts she heatin up the coffee over the Sterno. Soon as I walk in they all start talkin. Mission say. "Whut I want to know is who get his comic books?" An the others all askin questions like who gets the close for they kid brothers an like that.

"Comic books stay here." I tell them. "Little Mans comic books belong to the Club now. The close you can divide up among the ones who got kid brothers an Lu Ann can have the shirt she wearin an 1 or 2 more."

Lu Ann say. "That all they is. 1 or 2 more is all he got."

The boys go inta Little Mans room an clean out the closet an the draws an divide up his close in little piles on the bed. I pick up all the comic books layin aroun an bring them in to the kitchen. The guys have brought up chairs people throwed out on the street an our Club room look like it beginnin to shape up.

Lu Ann grab the 2 shirts that look pretty good an take them inta the front room. Mission and the other

134

guys they wrap up what they divide in news paper an take it home. I tell them. "You be sure to show here to night. We got some work to do gettin the armory in shape."

Soon as the door close Lu Ann say to me. "Duke you wasnt kiddin was you? You gonna take me to that iland tomorra to see the ocean?"

"I give you my word dint I?"

She come over an sit in my lap an put her skinny arms aroun me. "I bin sittin here all this time wonderin how come no body ever tol me about it befor that the ocean was out on the end of the subway."

Her skin so cool an smooth. I touch her all over under her shirt an evry where. She kiss me on the mouth. "You a sweet man Duke." She say. "I owe you 1 from last night if you want it."

So I stay with Lu Ann an other 1 hour or so but all the time I thinkin how I should get up to Priests place an try to get the piece from him with some money down an the rest later. Lu Ann tellin me that day how she love me.

I make the down payment

I knock at the door at Priests apartmint. The door got this iron flandge on it so you cant jimmy it open. People either got the flandge or they got a dog but that dont stop the robbin. The robbin go on an if you got the flandge an a dog both you still aint safe from havin you place broke in. I knock at the door an Priest crack it open on the chain. He give a big smile.

"Duke Man. Nice to see you." He say. "Uh Duke now I got a client here. Give me five ten minutes. Can you wait?"

I sit down on the bottom step of the stairs goin up to the roof an start to wait. Waitin always make me itchy. The hall floor made out of tiles. White tiles with six sides like a diamond thats flat on the top an the bottom. Priests bildin is kept pretty good the super mop the floors at lease once a week. An all the apartments have they own toilet so you dont have to go out in the hall an wait you turn.

I start to think about whut I have got to do in the way of things for the Club. Theys the armory got to be taken care of so evry body got arms when we go down on the Wolves. An tonight when I see the guys I got to tell some of them who I pick for it that they are scouts. Send them inta Wolves territory to scout an see where they hangin out these days an whut kind of strenth they got. Lot of other things. You got to take the reesponsibilities when you President. People think it all glory but it aint.

Finely Priests door open an a man in a slick gray suit slip out an go down the stairs not lookin left or right an keepin his head down. Priest stick his head out an say. "Duke?" I go on in. Priest set down in his chair.

"Sorry to keep you waitin Duke." He say. "What can I do for you?"

"Oh Man what can you do for me. You know why I here Priest."

Priest laugh an that chair of his snicker an snitter along with him like it laughin too. "Man you still interested in that little old piece of mine? That old thing still got you eye Duke?"

"If you still got it Priest why I ready to talk money with you." I say.

"Oh I still got it." He say. "You come to the right place Man for whut you want."

"How I know it work?" I ask him.

"They aint but one way of findin out Duke. You gotta test it. An if you aint satisfied with the action why Man jus bring it back an get you money back. Thats the way I do bisness."

He sit there like a rock. You cant move him you know. I dont even try to talk price with him. He name it at 15 an he wont take 14.99. Priest got a rep for fair dealin. He trust worthy. He bin in bisness at the same place for a long time an that always a good sign. He been a year now that I know of.

I say. "Now Priest. At this moment I got a certain amount of cash but the 15 if I pay it out all at once is gonna leave me pretty low."

"You wanta leave a deposit?" He ask me.

"Thats whut I been thinkin Priest. That I leave you say 5 then I be back next week some time with the 10."

Priest say. "Unh huh." His eyes roll back in his head you know to show he thinkin. "I dont run no lay away department store Duke. This a strictly what they call Cash An Carry bisness."

"I need the piece Priest Man an I am no in an out drifter. I a steady naborhood boy an you always know where to find me."

"Lets see the 5 Duke." He say.

I show it to him. He take it an while he lookin at me he fold it up 40 times till it jus about disapeer inta nothin at all an then he tuck it away in his watch pocket. "I makin an ex ception for you Duke."

"You still got the piece Priest? I want the one I look at last time."

Priest tap the draw with his nuckel. "It right here where you saw it last." He say. He fold his hands in his lap an he say. "Duke I know this here trans action is gonna be kep between jus you an me."

I say smilin. "Who Priest?"

"Thats whut I like to hear." He say.

"Man." I say. "I sure would like to handle the piece for a minute. Want to get the feel of it."

"Duke I expectin a big customer any minute now." He smile. "Dont you worry about a thing. The piece in workin order." He tap the draw with his nuckel. "It yours Duke. Got you name on it now." He tap the draw. Goes thum thum thum.

I go. I slip out the door an lookin not right or left hurry down the stairs like the guy in the slick gray suit done befor me. I thinkin. "Watch out now.

Watch out now all you Wolves. Here come one of Priests customers. Stan back or get burned." An my hand go all hollow you know feelin the coolness of the piece in it. An when I step out on the street I know any body lookin at me know that I am a man who have the power.

The new crocadiles

When I get back up to the Club house I find Saint an Lu Ann havin a fight over the comic books. Saint sayin they belong to the Club an Lu Ann aint no full member of the Club an she cant have the comic books. Lu Ann keep pullin at the books from Saints hand an sayin all about how she got her rights.

"Rights you aint got no rights." Saint say. "The ony right you got is to keep 1 dollar out the price thats the ony right you got."

Lu Ann say. "Leggo or I tare them. How you like that you bastard an then no one can read them. I swear to GOD if you dont leggo Saint I gonna rip them a part."

Saint he finely let go. He could see she ment it. Lu Ann dont fool aroun says somethin she mean it.

Saint let go an Lu Ann had them. "I bring them back soon as I finish with them." She say.

Saint say. "You makin more money than the rest of us why dont you go out an buy you own books stead of readin off the Clubs."

Lu Ann say to Saint. "Dont come aroun *here* with any of that you aint a member shit Man." She say an walk out the room.

When we alone Saint laugh. "She the toughest little wiry girl I ever met up with. Where she come from any way? Who is she any way?"

"I dont know. She just here." I tell him.

"Well it dont matter to me." He say. "I can take them or not take them. I dont mind a girl like Lu Ann who know whut it all about an dont think she so goddam important jus because she a girl like some of those girls we uset to have aroun in the old days. Remember that Duke Man? The trouble we had in the old days when we had the Debs?"

The Debs was the ladys auxilary of the Crocadiles for a while in the old days. That was when Blood was full of heart an we was a fightin gang. It dint last long. The Debs was always aroun. Evry day some one of them girls would come aroun an say. "Blood I jus saw a member of the Wolves an I dint like the way he look at me." Or one come in an say. "A Wolf jus come up to me in the street an he say you chicken Blood." So then we round up the guys an go down on the Wolves. Half the time the Debs jus make up the story because then they could act important. Also they like the rumbles because then they could come along with us.

It go like this. We move in to Wolves territory two or three in a grupe so the headbreakers wont know somethin up. Evry guy got a girl along with him she carryin his weapon so that if the headbreakers pick him up why they got to let him go because he aint armed. Then when we get close to the Wolves the girls pass us the weapons an wait aroun till after the rumble over. After the rumble over if we aint on the run or dead we pass the weapon back to the girl an she hide it out for us till things cool down.

An also they like whut happen after the rumble. After the rumble we always have this big party the guys that have made it. We have wine at lease an some time wiskey also. No matter whut happen in a rumble if you alive after it over you the winner. Same time we havin our party the Wolves prolly havin one also. So the guys whut have made it usely have this victory celebration. The girls get all excited because they can smell the victory on us an that make them all excited.

At those partys they a lot of screamin an music an

dancin. Some times a brawl even though the guys all banged up an you think tired of fightin for one day. But the wine and the wiskey revive them. When you young like that like we was in the old days I writin about here now it dont take much to revive you when you down. Some time we have the party in some girls house who mother work nights or maybe she over in Brooklyn or some where takin care of a sick mother or sister or somethin like that.

We get the radio goin with disk jockey music an start dancin. Some dancin an others drinkin an soon the Debs start laughin sound like screamin. Once I see one Deb the wiskey took her in such a way that she was like froze. Coulden move. Jus stood there ridgid an evry now & then she moan. Wildman those victory parties. People layin aroun all over the place beds an floor an evry where. Some sleepin it off an some makin out.

Some times I uset to sit there with a glass in my han an jus look at whut goin on an I think. "Man if the Mother walk in now whut a cry she raise. Man if the Mothers knew half whut goin on they go crazy." Some do find out. Some bound to find out soon or later. Usely then they move. They take the girl to a new place in Brooklyn or Queens or some where like they think changin the neiborhood gonna make some difference. Neiborhoods all the same.

Once in a while a girl get in real trouble you know. Cherokees brother he uset to be in the gang an this girl had a Father he made Cherokees brother marry her. She was 15 an had to have her parents permission. Cherokees brother he quit school and marryed her. Quit the gang. We dont hardly ever see him no more. He come aroun evry once in a while for old time sake. Workin in a sheet metal place downtown some where.

One guy I know his family foun out he runnin with the gang an about the drinkin an all an they moved way the hell an gone to some place called Gary. Its past Philly he told us. They a lot of comin an goin on the street but the gang up to full strenth all the time. We got about 50 they always ready for a fight with the Wolves. Bein in the gang gives you a lot of whut they call statis. Lot of guys they jus hang aroun till finely they elected in to the club. Lately with Blood the way he is they aint even no elections. Guy hang aroun with us for a while an then one day he jus in. He a member. Gangs dont last long when that begin to happen. Let evry body in an the gang get big but it the reputation that make a gang strong an feared by the other gangs.

Talkin to Saint about the old days an whut happen to the gang with Blood lettin things go bad. I tell

Saint. "Lot of things need changin aroun here an I gonna make some changes."

"We with you on that Duke." Saint a good man got a lot of heart. "They a new spirit in the gang since you become President. Cowboy an Rod pullin blades is a sign. Its a sign that things is changin aroun here. That the first fight in a long time an it show the new spirit. Evry body behin you Duke Man."

"Saint." I say. "I namin you Gunsmith. I want the Armory to be got in shape."

Saint say. "Duke you got you self a Man."

I tell him. "I want evry thing polished an sharp an GI."

"I get on it right away Duke."

"You find you self some pencil an paper an make a list. So we know whut we got."

Saint go in Little Mans room an take the Armory out from under the bed an he go to work. I can hear the stuff clashin an thumpin on the floor. He layin it out to make the count. I sit there in the kitchen with a glass of muscatel an wait for the guys to show. Lu Ann come in with 3 comic books. She say to Saint as she passin thru Little Mans room. "Here you lousy books. I finish 3 of them already." She come in to where I am an put the books down on the table.

"Dont forget tomorra Duke." She say to me.

I tell her. "All right now. I promise to take you an I takin you. Dont be botherin me with it evry minit. I got a lot on my mind right now."

"OK Duke." She say. "You gonna stay here tonight with me Duke?" She say then.

"I let you know."

"Duke you got any smokes for me?"

"No more. I got to sell all I got. When I raise the money for the piece I start fixin you up again. But right now I need all the bread I can get."

She go up front an come back an put five ones on the table. "Sell me 5 Lover." She say. "You know I help you all I can."

I tuck the five away an give her the smokes. "You all right Lu Ann." I say.

"I see you later Duke honey." She say. "OK?"

I say OK. She go up front then an smoke I guess. She get a lot of plesure out of it. I never see any body pull down the smoke like Lu Ann like she drinkin it. She suck it down inta her lungs an hold it there takin these little breaths to keep the smoke in. She always say. "You got to get it into you blood streem or it dont do you half as much good." She know evrythin about it I dont know where she learned it.

After a while the place fill up. Rod an Cowboy come in an evrybody keepin an eye out on them. But the cool is on an they gettin along all right. I tell them I got Saint makin a count on the Armory. An I tell 3-4 of the guys that from now on they Snakes. Snakes is the name we got for runners you know the guys that snake in an out of Wolves territory an bring back reports an take messeges. I send out a couple Snakes that night an tell them to keep they eyes open an stay outa trouble. "You job is to come back with the report." I tell them.

Rod say. "That a good thing you doin Duke man. We need reports. We dont have any idee no more of what they strenth is."

Cowboy say. "They got a worker from the Youth Board so they must be pretty strong."

Saint walk in to the room lookin important with a piece of paper in his hand. Bishop get up from the table an Saint sit down. I say. "War Council now meetin. Saint got a report on the Armory."

Evry body get quiet. Saint look at his paper. He say. "I got a report here on the Armory. This whut we got. We got 22 blades 3 blackjacks 5 zip guns an no bullets an we got 6 cutlasses an a bunch of radio aireals."

"Whuts the condition of the blades?" Rod says.

"They OK." Saint say.

"We need more blades." I tell them. "I want more

blades for the in fightin. An I want a lot more of the aireals for the charge. I plan it this way. We go in slashin with the aireals an when they fall back we go for them with the blades. Also we got to get up some bread for ammo for the zips. If you go in burnin it give you an edge." An that the truth you know. The sound of a gun put fear in them no matter how much heart you have or how long a time you been swingin with the gangs. Its the sound means Death near by. Dyin is easy but takin the charge is real hard.

I know because I seen it an the fact I never tol any body not even any members of the Crocadiles dont mean I dint see it. When you see a thing like that I mean a reaì killin with death involved it better to keep you mouth shut for good an all. But I was there that time 3 guys came in an found a certain man in the number bisness sittin at the bar in a certain candy store.

I was sittin in the back an saw them in they big shouldered coats walken in out of the cold with they breath steamin out of them. They dint look at any one thing but the number man. He the one an they dont see nothin else like nothin else dint exist. The 3 of them came up to that man an one of the 3 say. "Hello John." John aint really his name. He say. "Hello John." John dont turn aroun because he sees him in the mirrur an his head sorta sink down inta his shoulders.

The one man say. "Dont you have a word for us John?" An when John still dont say anythin they give it to him. They standin behin him like in a triangle you know an they blaze away. Papers say 12 bullets in him but I lost count. No body could count them as they burned because it all too fast. They burned him an he fell to the floor like somethin wet. An the one that doin the talkin say to the candy store man. "You was in the back an you dint see anythin."

I cleared out fast an up to until this day no body know I was a witness to that certain killing. Doc Levine you are the first to know.

So thats how I say I know I know whut a gun can do not only to the man who gets the charge but also to them whut only witness an hear it.

I say to Saint. "Well you done a good job of it Saint. Lets go take a look at it." An we went inta Little Mans old room an Saint had the stuff spread out on the floor. Rod lit a candel an we examined the blades an things an it was all like Saint say it is in pretty good shape. I picked up a cutlass an took a swipe with it. It got a nice grip on it. We got these cutlasses from some members who found a smashed up crate down near the docks one day an in the crate they foun these cutlasses. The crate belong to the U.S. Navy but no body know who the cutlasses belong to. An if you return a thing like 6 cutlasses it cant do you any good with the cops. They dont thank you for it but only ask a lot of questions.

The cutlass I holdin still got this black tassell on it at the handel. It a real sporty lookin piece. Cowboy say. "Man you look like Earl Flynn." An then we hear the kitchen door slam an then we hear Bloods voice sayin. "Where Duke?"

I give the sign to Rod an Cowboy an they step inta the kitchen right behind me an I say. "Blood we tole you oncet to stay away from here."

He put out his hand. His face all fallin apart. He say. "Uh uh uh uh Duke now Man uh uh. Lissen now uh Duke Man."

Behin me I hear Rod say. "He need a fix bad." An Cowboy say. "Yeh."

I put the point of the cutlass on the floor an I say. "Now Blood no body want any trouble with you. They nothin for you here any more."

Then he say to me. "Uh uh uh now Duke Man now lissen uh uh. Uh all I need Duke man all I need uh uh is some bread uh maybe 2-3 dollas Duke Man."

"You took all the money we got Blood. We dont have no more for you."

151

"Throw him out Duke." Cowboy say. "Or let me do it for you Man. Throw the junkie out he aint nothin but trouble now."

"Nothin but nothin now." Some body say.

Blood cryin. Tears rollin down his face his face all wet with tears. "Man." He say to me. "Like Man uh uh Man I need it bad Man. Duke Man."

"Nothin here for you now Blood." I say. "Time to go." An I signal to Bebop to open the door. He standen behin Blood an an he open the door. "Time to go Blood."

Blood cryin an sayin. "Uh uh uh Duke uh uh Man. Uh Man Duke uh uh."

I take him by the arm an spin him aroun facin the door an give him a little push. He still talkin not sayin any thing. He try to come back an I push him against the wall an let go of him. I stan with my back to the door an the stairs on my left an watch him. He put out his hand one more time an he say. "Lissen Duke Man lissen. Uh uh uh." The guys all standen in the door watchin him. I shake my head no an Blood start for the stairs. He all bent over with the cramps. His hand reach for the railin an he miss it an his foot miss an he go right down those stairs fallin head over heels. No body push him.

I went to the stairs an saw him land at the bottom

152

on hands an knees. He got a cut acrost his for head an the blood comin down his face. He look up at me standen there with the cutlass. He dont say a word but he kinda moanin from his mouth an then he start crawlin away down the hall.

I stand there thinkin about his brother down at Fisk an that day I saw him in his Mothers house. The day they sent Blood with money to the super market an he never come home an they sittin in that room fulla books wonderin where John Wesley where is he gone. I remember that day an I think well John Wesley you finely made it you an animal at last. You a complete animal.

We go to Coney

Some time I jus dont under stand Lu Ann an how she acts I mean. All the time we in the subway she actin like a scared little kid who aint never been in a subway befor. She keep crowdin up to me an holdin onto my arm an puttin her head on my shoulder. She say. "Oh Duke I dont like this bein under ground like this."

I say. "We be out of it soon."

"When?" She say. "Nex stop Duke? Will we be out of it nex stop?"

People lookin at her the way she huddlin up against me like she cold or somethin an wantin to get warm. I keep tryin to move away a little but the train too crowded. Jammed with people carryin bags fulla bathinsuits an sanwiches & carryin portable radios an even portable fonografs. Babys cryin an kids yellin an 1 old man sittin there readin a newspaper with funny printin on it like he all by him self. Lu Ann keep lookin at this old man with the long white beard.

She say. "Whuts that crazy printin he readin off that newspaper?"

"Look like Chineese to me." I tell her.

"You gassin me Duke?"

"It could be Chineese." I tell her. "An stop crowdin me."

"I dont like it down here Duke."

"Well aint nothin I can do about it Lu Ann. You want to see the goddam ocean this the way how you got to go to get there." I say to her an pull my arm away from where she clutchin at it.

She hunch her self an say. "Dont be mean to me Duke." An then she sit there like she goin to cry. I never see her like that befor. Next stop she clutch my arm again an then I notice like you know evry time the train stop at a stop she grab my arm. She thought I gonna run out on her.

Lu Ann sit thru the whole rest of the ride with out she sayin a word an not takin her eyes off the old man with the white beard readin the newspaper. Evry once in a while he make his hand into like a komb an komb his beard but keep on readin that crazy newspaper an never raisin his eyes from it.

Lu Ann say. "Is it the nex stop yet Duke?" An I swear to it whut happen then. The old man never lift his eyes but he like knew. He started foldin his paper. He folded it into a square like it was a hankercheef an stuck it in his pocket. An jus the second he finish doin it the train came out of the ground and the sun come in! Lu Ann look at me. That old man knew right to the second! Lu Ann never took her eyes off him an I kep lookin at him. When we got out the train he was right in front of us wearin this crazy black coat an hat even in all that hot wether. An then he jus disapeer. Goin down the steps. Suddenly he gone an no where though we look aroun evry where.

When we get to the bottom of the steps Lu Ann take my arm ahold so tight I stop an look at her. She lookin at me her eyes all round like she jus found money. She say. "You know who that was Duke?"

"Who?"

"The old man." She say. I knew she ment the old man. I say. "I know the old man. Who is he?" An she say. "Duke he must be GOD that old man."

"Oh Man." I say an hit my for head to show her how crazy an wild she is.

"No now Duke lissen Man." She say. "He got that beard like GOD dont he? An he readin that crazy print no body know how to read. An he knew when we was comin out from under ground dint he? Knew it befor any body an with out even lookin up. Now aint that all true Duke?"

I say yeh I guess that all true.

Lu Ann say. "Well then. He GOD all right. No body else he could be."

"Oh Man you really wild." I say. "You been smokin too much Lu Ann."

"He GOD." She say. "I tellin you Duke an I know it. Man that old man is GOD."

I say to her. "So if he GOD you tell me whut he doin here on a hot day like this ridin the train to Coney." Is whut I say to her.

"May be he come out to see the ocean." She say.

I take her arm an start walkin her again. "You real wild Lu Ann. He invent the ocean so why would he come all this way to see it?"

She say. "How I know why he come all this way. Man jus cause he invent it dont mean he dont ever want to see it. Duke Man whuts that crazy smell?"

I tell her. "Thats the ocean you smellin. We almost to it now. That the board walk up ahead. We go up on the board walk an you can see it."

She start takin long deep breathes like she smokin an tryn to get it in to her blood streem. "Smell like fish." She say. "Smell like cold fish an salt."

"That whut the ocean is." I tell her. "Fulla salt an fish."

"You gassin me Duke?"

"Oh Man." I say.

We walk up this like little rise an on up to the board walk. Jammed with people. I take Lu Anns arm an snake our way thru till we up against the rails on the other side. "Well they it is Lu Ann. I promise you an I keep my promise now look at it."

She look at it. "Oh Man." She say. "It always movin like that Duke all the time? It never stop? Duke Man I wanta get down there close to it.

I take her under the board walk an out on the sand. Soon she stop an take off her shoes an we go walkin aroun all the people layin out tryin to get black on towels. Lu Ann hurryin ahead like she forget all about me an I tryin to keep up with her without I step on some body. We get to the part of the beech where the sand damp an Lu Ann keep walkin till the ocean come in an wet her feet. "That water cold." She say. Nex wave come by she stick her hand in it an taste the stuff. "Man you wasnt gassin me." She say. "That salt all right." She stand there I dont know how long lookin out an lettin them little waves scutter over her ankels.

She say "Duke whut happen when you get out there

158

to where it end? Out to where that line is Duke."

"Thats Europe out that way." I tell her.

She look at me like she goin crazy. "An which way to Africa Man?" She ask me.

"Well you go out a ways an then you head south." I dont know for sure about that but I figure it hot in Africa so it prolly south. Lu Ann stand there lookin out like she gonna see both them countries any minit. She say. "Duke when I look down at my feet when the ocean come in it look like I goin out. Hold onto me Duke."

"You aint goin no where. That jus the tide pullin at you." I say.

Two little Negro kids whut have been in swimmin a boy an a girl maybe 7 year old come walkin in holdin hands an Lu Ann say to them. "Childern do you know thats Europe an Africa out there?"

The little boy say. "Sure we know that." An they keep on walkin.

I gettin tired of standin an my shoes full of sand. I say. "Lu Ann I tired of standin. Lets go get a hot dog an take some rides."

"I dont want to go yet." She say.

"We gonna come back." I say. "Come on now. We get some hot dogs an go on some rides."

Finely she come with me talkin all the time about

the ocean an Europe out there an all that. We eat some hot dogs Lu Ann payin an then I took her on some rides. We went on the whip an rode risin horses on the merry go round an all like that. The big ones. Lu Ann aint much intrested in them. So after a while an it was gettin late I sit her down on a bench an tell her to wait I have to find the toilets.

When I come back she gone. I sit down an wait. I figure she prolly went to find the toilets too. I wait a long time an then I think she prolly down on the beach standin in the ocean again so I go down to look for her.

I look all up an down that beech for her an callin her name. Woman say to me. "Boy you lookin for a little girl?" I say yes an she say. "Well they was a little lost girl an the cop took her to the station. About 7-8 year old?" She say. I tell her no that aint the one I lookin for.

Then when it get dark I walk up an down the board walk an even went thru the fun house an the tunnel of love. I stand out side the shows an the horror museums an lookin for her evry where till near mid night it was. I knowed she would never find her way home with out me. But I never find her.

I wait for her all night in the front room at Little Mans. Two or 3 time in the night I think I hear her comin. "Lu Ann." I say. "Lu Ann. That you Lu Ann?"

But in the morning she wasnt there an the nex day an the nex day neither. So finely I know she aint comin back an that she lost for good. She had her pocket book with her an I guess all the money she made. I dont know whut ever happen to her. May be she go to San Francisco. No body I know of ever see her again.

Whut happen at Royals

The day after Coney was a Monday first day of the big week. Knew in my bones when I woke up it was goin to be the Big Week. After I wake up I lay on the bed a minit an like see my self layin there. Like I up on the ceelin lookin down at my self on the bed. They he is. Duke Custis. President of the Crocadiles. Layin aroun in his own club house that has an inside toilet an evry thing. Got a good job an money in his pocket. 5 dollas down paid restin easy at Priests an the piece almost mine. I look at my self layin there an I say right out loud. "Man you got it made."

I get up an make some of Lu Anns coffee on the Sterno an sit drinkin it at the kitchen table. Makin plans. The way the guys all revved up I know we should go down on the Wolves soon. Befor they go cool. If you have too much time to think about a rumble why then you got time to get scared. It a scary time no matter how many time you been in on one. You start thinkin about the blades an the aireals swishin thru the air. Zip guns an sawd off shot guns an the clubs goin for you head. Some reason I always worry about gettin it in the head.

But this time I aint worried. I feelin good about evry thing. That mournin I still think maybe Lu Ann find her way back. But she never did. Dont know to this day whut happen to her. Maybe some day I get to San Francisco an look for her that crazy kid the way she uset to lay there on the bed sayin. "San Fran cis co San Fran cis co."

At that time that day I tellin you about now the sun shinin an I figure I dont have a worry in the world. Evry thing goin my way an Man I got it made. The spirit good in the Crocadiles. An this time at last the Wolves sittin an wait for us. They the ones this time to do the scared an tremblin.

Because I know the signs. I know the signs an when a gang start with the ambushes an jappin a man in his own hallway an tryin to run him down with a car why Man that a sign that the gang comin apart. It always work that way. When a gang a real tight boppin outfit they come in strong an not 2 3 or 6 at a time. When a gang fallin apart an the spirit an fight gone why then they start with the gorilla kind of fightin.

So knowin that an knowin the spirit in my own men I know the time is now an sooner the better. I decide it then an they at the table by my self. Friday night or Saturday night we go down on the Wolves.

Evry thing be ready then got to be ready then. The Armory got to be shape up an I got to have my piece. Right then I had 3 dollas of my own in my pocket. I figure I can sell in 3 days easy another 36 smokes. That give me 9 an 3 which make 12. I owe Priest 10 an then the piece mine an I got 2 dollas lef for buyin ammo. Set. An I go inta Wolves turf burnin an come walkin out with a big name for my self.

So after I finish breakfass I go down to the street an even that street smell good to me. I bounce a little on my heels an sayin "How you? How you?" to people sittin on stoops. I go aroun the block so as not to have to go past my own house. Dont want no more talk from Hurst. Dont want to see my Mother neither. At this time now I aint been home for 3 day an dont want to get mix up with my Mother. She know I aroun the neiberhood she can report me to the Youth people like she say she gonna do. An this aint no time to get involve with the Youth people an like that.

I make it to Lexington with out bein seen by any

body whut matter. I walk past the gypsys store an she sittin in the door with that baby of hers. She call to me. "Boy." She say. "Boy come here." I went over. I got a good look but Man she dont care. Baby suckin away with one little hand on her tit like it glued there. She say. "You got any money today Boy because this a good day for makin a readin. You got a dolla an I give you a full compleet for cast."

I like to do it but the money tight an I thinkin about nothin in the way of money but the piece in Priests draw. So I tell her No I aint got a penny.

She say. "You get hold of a dolla for you self Boy an come back. Be the best dolla you ever spend. I give you a compleet an full for cast an you wont have nothin to worry about."

"I try to get it." I tell her jus to get away. I dont like to stand there watchin the baby eat. "I get the dolla I come back to day Missus."

"I dont cheat like other gypsies." She say.

"I know you dont."

She switch the baby aroun to the other one. Baby give one yelp an then he stop right away when he get the other one in his mouth. I never seen it close up be for.

"You come back Boy. I give you a readin an you will know the whole Future. You know the whole

Future evry wrinkel an shadow. You know whut the others dont know. Give you Power Boy. It give you Power to know whut the others dont know."

"You right about that." I tell her an start movin off I got a lot to do. "I get me the dolla an I come right back."

"All right Boy I wait for you." She say after me.

I go on up to Royals place. I knock an wait. Then I knock again. Finely the door open on the chain. It Miss Dewpont. She say. "Oh it you. Come on in." An she open the door.

This time she wearin a pink thing an when she walk ahead of me you can see the shadow of her legs thru it. She sit down on the sofa where she got a cup of coffee sittin on the arm. She get up as soon as she down an pick up the cup. "Come in the kitchen with me will you Duke an we have some coffee to gether. I do hate to drink alone."

So I folla her inta the kitchen watchin her legs move thru the flimy thing she wearin an wonder whut happen to Roy? How come he aint aroun? First time. She say. "Sit down Duke." An I sit down at the kitchen table. It have one of them cold white tops. Miss Dewpont pour me a cup of coffee an have another for her self.

I take a sip of it an say. "That real good coffee."

166

She smile an say. "Why thank you Kind Sir." She got a real little voice you know kinda like a little girls voice. Then she make her face all serious an she say. "I dont know how to tell you Duke. I dont rightly know how to break the news to you."

"Royal get picked up?" I ask her.

She say. "Duke I got bad news for you. Royal got picked up lass night. I ony heard about it jus by chance thru some kind friends who saw it happen in a certain bar down the street where Royal go evry evenin to meet some dear friends of his who are also in bisness. Various lines of bisness."

"That sure is too bad." I say. But all I thinkin about is the piece in Priests draw an how it look like I never goin to get my hand on it.

"You a sweet young lad." She say an pat my hand. "I mean to take it so personal like. Royal always say he feel like a Father to you."

I keep my hand there on the table along side my coffee cup but she dont touch it again.

I say. "Well I dont suppose Royal lef any supplies aroun an you could let me have 12 more smokes?"

"Well I dont rightly know Duke." She say. Then she say. "Well I suppose the work mus go on. I look aroun an see whut I can find."

I take out the 9 dollars for the last 12 smokes that I

167

owe Royal Poinciana an pass it across the table to her. She tuck it inta a pocket. She say. "I know that Royal gonna apresheate you loyalty. We both very fond of you Duke an expectin big things."

I say. "Well it too bad it had to happen to Royal."

"Oh." She say. "Well I guess that the risk you have to take when you are performin services for others."

"Things been cool a long time." I say.

"Yes." She say. "Royal been expectin it. He get picked up regular about once a year. Some body up on top dont pay off or somethin happen you know an then they pick up where they can. Royal have got picked up a few times but they always let him go because they dont have any evidence."

Her white hand layin on the white top of the table. "Royal smart." I say.

"Royal always say If you run a tight shop they never get you for good."

"How long they keep him?" I thinkin about the piece an how I need the smokes to get up the bread for the piece.

"Royal be so pleased to hear of you concern an solitude Duke." She say. "It a rare thing in a boy you age. Just how old exacly are you Duke?"

"Uh 16." I say. Some times I say 14 an some times

16 an other times 18 so I had to stop & think befor I said it that I was 16.

"16." She say. "I swear Duke I thought you was 18 if a day."

I tell her. "Lot of people take me for 18. Because I so tall I guess."

She look at me an smile an say. "How you like an other cup of coffee Duke? Boy like you ought to eat good." She pour me more coffee. I dont really want it but I dont say anythin. She say. "I am sorry Duke that I dont have cake to offer you. I bet you like somethin sweet with you coffee dont you?"

"This jus fine." I tell her.

"Most boys do like sweet sticky things." She say. She lookin at my hand on the table an I dont say nothin but wait for her. Finely she say. "You hand so beautiful on the white table." I look at my hand. She put her hand along side my hand. "Now it even more beautiful." She say her voice all shaky an trembly. The edge of her hand jus touchin the edge of my hand an she start slidin her hand back an forth. "You know whut Duke?" She ask me.

"Whut?" I say.

She say. "They nothin more excitin in the whole world than black skin against white skin."

169

I never thought about it befor. I jus sat stiff in my chair an watchin her hand move against my hand an her head fallin lower an lower wonderin whut she gonna do now. She bend way down an kiss my hand. Miss Dewpont got bright yella hair somethin like a canary. One of those birds you know.

When she pick up her head her eyes all funny an her mouth hangin open. I can hear her breath an under her eyes her skin gone all blue. She say like a whisper. "Dont be scared of me Duke."

I tell her I aint scared but my legs are shakin. I follaed her into her room an it was like when I went to the Park with Rod. I mean that the way I felt the same way. I dint know whut to say to her & I dont know whut she wanted from me. I jus try to folla an guess an keep up with her an when she take off her flimy robe I taken off my close also. Then I lay down on the bed aside her but not touchin.

She put her leg along side mine an like that. Touchin me all along the side. She roll her head aroun an whisper. "Oh Christ look at that did you ever see any thing so beautiful. Look at us Duke. Oh look at us an tell me if you ever see anything so beautiful in all you life."

It like one of them crazy times when I like up on the ceelin you know lookin down at my self. It like the Fun House at Coney. Real scary you know. She got this mirra up on the ceelin over the bed an I dint reelize it at the first. I dint know whut it was. First I thought it was one of those crazy times when I at 2 places at one time an the same. Then I see me an her in the mirra up on the ceelin layin there side by side an not movin except her head.

"Look at us Duke." She whisper. "You ever see anything like it?"

I tell her No I never have seen. She put her hand on my chest an legs an evry where an watch it in the mirra lookin up evry time she move her hand. Miss Dewpont a skinny woman but not skinny like Lu Ann because she older. She dont have the kinda tight body Lu Ann got. She take my hand an put it on her an hold it there tight against her. "Dont move." She say. "Dont move now." An her body go all stiff pressin against my hand. In the mirra our hands like a black an white X. Her eyes wide open lookin at her self with the blue smudges under them. Blue an like purple at the edges. "Harder." She say. "Dont be scared." An she almos lift her self off the bed pushin against my hand. Then she get all crazy rollin her head an her yellow hair all over her face. She breathin an cryin like she in trouble an holdin my hand like she gonna break my wrist. Then she let go of me finely an get all limp. I watch her in the mirra not lookin at her self. Jus lookin at her self in the mirra. Evry time she breath her hair move thats all over her face. She lay there a long time.

Finely she move her legs. Then she lift her arm an push her hair away an look at me lookin at her in the mirra. She say. "You aint scared of me are you Duke?" An I tell her again No. She say. "You see Duke it just that I worried about Royal. An I know that Royal gonna apreesheate you loyalty when he get out. I think we oughta keep this jus between you an me Duke even though nothin really happen. You know how people are. Lot of people jus dont under stand how pure an sweet a thing can be. I guess you have notice that. They are always people who like to think the worse of evry body. Any one seein us here would know how pure & sweet we are but the people who dont see us why they the very ones you got to watch out for. You see what I mean?"

"Yes Mam." I say. But she aint listenin.

"People dont under stand I tell you Duke. Black & white is all the same as far as under standin go. People like to think whuts bad an they dont stop to think whuts good. For me its bein happy an breakin thru thats whut count. I have try to be happy with my own kind an break thru with my own kind but Duke I

172

jus cant make it. When you cant make it with you own kind then you have to break thru with the kind whut you can break thru with be they whut ever color they may be." She take my hand an hold it but very soft now. "You got eyes Duke." She say. "You look aroun you see I not the only one who found the way to break thru. They a lot of us an we no worse then some of those down town who just dreamin about it an dont have the nerve for it."

I dont know whut to say to her. She talkin wild like I never hear any one talk befor. I let her hold my hand an I nod an say Uh huh but I dont do any talkin.

Finely we get out of bed an I get dress. She say. "I look aroun Duke an see whut I can find for you in the way of supplies." An she come back then with 12 smokes an give them to me. "These here the last supplies in the house Duke. Maybe Royal be out tomorra an we get some more."

"I hope so." I tell her.

She say. "I cant wait to see Royal an tell him whut a good lad he got in you." She put the 12 smokes in my pocket an say. "I guess I shouldnt give you evry last one thats in the house but I like you Duke because you loyal an because you under stand."

"Sure." I say.

"Some people." She say an she go thru that whole bisness again. I stand there itchin to go. Man I got so much to do it give me a head ache to think about them all. But I listen to her an nod an say Uh huh an like that. Then she give me a kiss on my cheek like I a little kid or somethin an open the door for me. "People dont under stand." She say. "How sweet & pure it is."

The wolves waitin

In those days in that week I tellin you about I uset to walk the street like I own it. Like in a western that man come inta town an no body know who he is. Got two silver guns an a black suit an boots. Walks down them wood payments like they had in those days an evry body look at him wonderin Who is he? Where he come from? Whut he want? He a man who know how to take care of him self that whut he is. An that whut I am. I a man who know how to take care of him self.

In fronteer days a man out West had to do evry thing for him self. An I uset to walk down 116 Street an you know aroun that neiborhood an it was my territory. It belong to me. Like in that movie The Baron of New Mexico. The King of Spain had give him New Mexico but then the Americans come an tell him it aint really his. He put up a fight but he lost.

Evry where in my territory that I walked those days I saw the signs of the rumble comein. Guys gave me the look an the sign with they hand an I could see that some of the girls knew it. I can tell by the way they say "Hi Duke Man" when I walk pass. Some of the old Debs they was who still runnin with some of the Crocadiles. An the coolies lookin at me scared but you know admirin an wishin they was with it though they glad they aint. When you out of somethin you always wish you was with it. That whut they call human nature.

That week when ever I move I move fast. I in a hurry for evry thing. Like when I pass the gypsys. I cross the street. I dont have time to stop an talk to her. She think I gonna make the fortune tellin a regular thing. But first of all I dint have the money to spare. An second of all when you think about it you know that they is a lot to it but it dont help you much to know the Future. I mean like she tell me a blond woman gonna give me bad news. OK. But they nothin you can do about it. You cant stop the blond woman from tellin you the bad news. Gypsy say I gonna be near the presense of Death. But you

cant stop Death. When you know the Future all it
do for you is make you worry. I wouldnt want to be
a gypsy.

I never have time for all whut I have to do that
week. Jus some of the things I have to do that week
is sell the smokes for the money for Priest an see to it
that evry man in the Crocadiles got arms. An that
mean goin to some body who aint in the gang an gettin
the loan of a blade or a few shells for the zips. Then
they is the money problem of rent time comin up on
the club house. Rent somethin you can put off for a
while but you cant put it off for ever. The super think
Little Mans father still livin in the apartment. Las
time we send down Little Man to pay the rent. This
next time we gotta send some body else an say to the
super. "Here the rent for Mister Tom Davis apartment."

When you get a rep an evrybody know you a man
who can take care of you self why then people start to
count on you an you have to take the reesponsibility.
Lotta guys I know back in the old days they coulda
been President steadof Blood but they dint want the
reesponsibility. You cant blame them. Some guys
ready for it an some guys aint.

Day I left Royal Barons apartment and that Miss
Dewpont I had a lot of things to do. I so bisy with

177

things to do I dint have the time to give much thought to Miss Dewpont an whuts with her. I dint think about it till a long time after when I had the time to think about it. Even when I had the time I wasnt able to figure it out whut it is with her. I have see a lot aroun here but I never see any thing like Miss Dewpont. She one of those whut they call a exciteable woman. You know whut they call nervus. She dont make sense. You cant figure her. Ony thing to do with a woman like Miss Dewpont is stay away. Dont see how Royal Baron put up with it excep he English an may be he dont know no better. He from the West Indys.

First thing I had to do was sell the smokes. I needed the money in my pocket. I mean I not worried about the headbreakers findin the stuff on me because I too fast for them. But I like the feel of the bread in my pocket because it mean the piece that much more mine an closer to my hand. So between leavin Barons an comin to our club house I manage to shake loose 4 coolies from a 1 dollar each leavin 8 to go. I get rid of the rest from among the members. Now with Lu Ann gone guys whut have some bread dont have to think about whut to blow it on. Weather Lu Ann or a smoke. Nothin to do now but smoke unless they knows some place else to buy some fur. You see a lot more new comic books aroun the club now that Lu Ann gone an the money freer.

First thing I do when I get up to the Club House I sit down at the table an I tell the Gunsmith an my War Lord an the Prime Minster to sit down at the table with me. Saint the Gunsmith. Rod is War Lord an Cowboy the Prime Minster. First thing we gotta do is get the reports from the Snakes.

I tell Cowboy I want the reports from the Snakes an he say. "All right you Snakes. Come over here an make you reports."

Warrior the first one up. He say. "The Wolves got this Worker from the Youth Board with them."

Evry body say. "We know they got the worker. They got the Worker 6 months now."

I slam my hand down on the table an evry body shut up. I look aroun at evry body an I say. "Let the man finish why dont you."

Warrior say. "One of the Wolves took a shot at the Worker yesterday an the headbreakers was all over the place even in the church."

"Did they kill him?" I ask Warrior.

"Jus graze him like." Warrior say.

Some body say. "Them Wolves cant shoot worth a damn."

Then they a young kid name Foxy. He uset to be

a friend of Little Man. Little Man brought him in to the club. He a Snake now. He come up to the table an take this little piece of chalk outa his shirt pocket. He say. "You see that piece of chalk? Well I tooken that piece of chalk with me last night inta Wolves territory. Took it right inta they own turf an wrote on the walls LITTLE MAN LITTLE MAN LITTLE MAN. Where ever I find a space I write his name. I let them know whut we revengin. Now all them Wolves settin in they Club House scared an tremblin knowin Little Mans revengers comin down on them."

"You did real good Foxy." I tell him. "Did you find out anything while you over in they territory."

He say. "I know a guy livin in the same house with a Wolve. He tell me most of them is on the junk. All the big shots. Angel an them guys they all on it."

Another Snake step up. He say. "It true. I got the word from a guy I know an he say the same thing."

Foxy say. "They aint takin the real stuff you know. They just usin that cheap 1 percent stuff."

Other kid say. "An 3 percent. I hear some of them takin up to 3 per cent."

"An the junk eaters still in the gang?" I ask them.

Foxy say. "Sure they still in the gang. They the leaders."

"I dont know whut happenin to the gangs." I say.

Cowboy say. "No it aint like the old days. Gangs all fallin apart lettin the junkies stay in. Half of em goin social runnin dances an things like that."

"They all got girls auxilarys." Rod say. "An then the Workers screwin things up. They bring in a ping pong table an evry body start runnin to the Worker with his troubles an befor you know it it all over. The boppin days is over an the girls is in an shitman." An Rod sit there with his mouth open but he dont say any more except swearin.

"We gonna go our own way doin whut we want to do." I tell them. "Dont you worry none about that. Any Worker come to us we get whut we can out of him an we dont give nothin at all. If he dont like it he can go down town an cry on the Mayors shoulder."

"At lease with the headbreakers you know where you stand." Cowboy say. "You know they out to get you."

I let them talk for a while an get rid of it all. Then I ask the Snakes if they got anymore to report. They say No. So then I ask how many blades been collected. Saint say he ony able to get 4 more that day an I tell the guys they gotta do bettern that. "You dont want to go down on the Wolves with out the right armamint do you?" I ask them. "Well Man get on it. We need the blades. I call this whole thing off if my men aint got the right equipmint."

They say. "No now Duke Man dont call it off. We get the stuff all right."

So I say. "Ok. It up to you. I cant do evry thing."

Saint say. "I pretty sure I can swing all we need by tomorra."

Saint the best Gunsmith the gang ever have. He got himself a little tablet an keepin a count of all the arms an he got 2 men to help him with the sharpenin.

Rod say. "Any body who aint provided him self with a blade by Saturday night can bring a kitchen knife. First rumble I in on I use my Mothers bread knife. Took it back an she never knowed the diffrence."

"Whut the War Lord say is right." Saint tell them. "A lot of you new men think you aint arm unless you got youself a Bowee knife or somethin like that. But you dont need no Bowee knife. All you need in a blade is that it got a cuttin edge an that it got a point. That all you need and dont you listen to anybody tell you diffrent."

I say. "That an order now. Any body dont have a blade by Saturday night bring him self a bread knife."

Then they all start talkin about knifes an Cowboy showin some of the kids how to use it the right way because some of them dont know how an the meetin

182

end. I get rid of the 8 smokes an I got 3 dollars more in my pocket all my own. An I thinkin You can have all the knifes you want. I gonna have my own piece an go down burnin.

I wonderin if Baron out yet an pray he is cause all I need all I need is another 12 smokes an I got it made. After that I can always rassle up the little bit I need. I say to Rod. "I gonna step out for a minit or 2. Need some air an hear whut I can hear. I be right back."

I go on down stairs an think about how I will go over to Ritzies Bar an see if any body there whut know if Baron out yet. I walk on over but no body in the Bar excep 2 men I never see befor drinkin beer. I ask the bar tender for Ritzie. He say. "She sold out. This my place now." He got a tight little squeeze up face an I see he got a big new sign up sayin how he dont serve any body who is a minor. I could tell him he aint gonna make a livin that way but he got the kind of face I know he wont listen. He the kinda bar tender who worry so much about losin his license he dont even notice till it too late all his customers has gone.

I go back to the Club house. The super settin on the stoop. "How you?" He say. "You a friend of Little Man aint you?"

I say yes.

He say. "If you goin up there now an if Mister Tom

Davis to home will you tell him the rents due."

"Sure. I tell him." I say.

"I been havin a lot of bad trouble with my legs or I go up there an tell him my self. Thats why I sittin out here on the stoop. Tryin to cool off my legs."

Old man with white hairs in his hair an he fool enough to look for a cool breeze in a Harlem summer. Man like that gonna wrassle garbage cans till he die. It make me sad to see an old man like that never got no where in all his life. Endin up with a room in the cellar. Gets his rent free an a few dollas more.

An goin up the stairs back to the Club House I think about Mister Tom Davis an Little Man an his brother in jail. Tom Davis. No body know where he is an he dont know even that Little Man dead. Little Man dead. The brother in jail. An he dont know his father disapeer an his little brother dead. He come out of jail in 10 year or so with good behavior an will he try to find his family? I dont know. If it was me maybe I would an maybe I wouldnt. It all depend. Most guys do. When they come out they come back an look for they family an friends. You see them aroun for a few days befor they go off some wheres else.

That whole family gone now. The mother an Little Man dead. Father gone. Brother in jail. Whole family shot to hell in no time at all. Thats the way it goes.

Baron & Priest

Next day I up so early it aint even hardly light out. But I so worryed whether Royal out that I cant sleep. I make my self coffee an then I come back up front with it because it misrable dark in the kitchen an real crummy with the candel futterin like it do. Like it breathin. I come back up front an sit down at the winda with my coffee. The sky comin blue an now you can see all the dirt an crap on the street.

No wind. It hot all ready. By the time an apartment just about start to cool off it start gettin hot again. When I was a kid I uset to think the heat dont come from the sun. I dint pay much attintion to the sun. I uset to think the heat come from the street an payments because they get so hot. Now I know it come from the sun but now it dont matter any more where it come from. It hot an that all that matter.

That whut I mean. I thinkin about this one day an I ask Doc. "Whut good is knowin?"

I sit at the winda an drink my coffee an look down at the street waitin for it to be time to go over to Barons apartment an see if he out. Man he got to be out! I thinkin. An I see myself with the price in my pocket walkin up the street to where Priest live. Walkin up the stairs and down the hall with the little white tiles on the floor. Knock at the door. Well Priest here I am. An I put the bread on the table. Priest say. Duke I never had a solidary doubt you could do it. He open the draw an hand me the piece. I unbutton my shirt an slip it under my belt. It dont make hardly any bulge at all.

Then the street dark an I standen in a door way an I hear the sound of attackin Wolves comin down. I step out real cool you know an walk out inta the middle of the street. I dont take out the piece yet. I keep my right hand up level with my belt an my arm bent.

When they see me they stop. 12 of them. Maybe 20. "Angel!" I say. "Angel! You a motheren yella bastard. Angel! You take shit from any body."

Then when he start to reach I pull my piece an burn. I put 3 holes in him an watch him slide. The other Wolves run away. I put the piece back in my

belt. Angel layin all over the street like. Spread out
you know all which ways like the dead do. The man
I saw get it in the lunchenette he look like some body
fold him like he was a piece of card board.

Angel say. "You got me fair Duke." An I walk away
slow & easy an disapeer into a bilding befor the headbreakers even wise to any thing happen.

I look out on that street jus gettin light with one
side the street light from the sun an other still dark.
Other side still in the shadow like night aint lifted
from it yet. An I see Death evry where. All a sudden
I seen Death evry where hidin in evry corner an doorway. Lookin out Death lookin out from behin evry
pole an winda an sign. Dont know why. Maybe it the
gypsy an whut she tell me.

An suddenly I get a feelin nothin gonna go right.
That it all gonna go bust. Suddenly I cant see nothin
ahead. Baron still in. No more smokes & no more
bread. No bread an no piece. I closed my eyes not to
see it all. Sat there with the cup in my hand an my
eyes closed I dont know how long. Because I thinkin
if I open my eyes I see Priest laughin at me. An hear
him sayin. "I sorry Duke but if you aint got the bread
you dont get the piece. I come from Spartacus Georgia an I dont aim to go back."

Finely I feel the sun on my knees an know the line

187

is gone an the street all light with out the shadow. I go down. I look left & right befor I step off the stoop. I smell the air an cant smell any thing to make me worry. I say to my self. "Man you had a bad minute. That all it was. A bad minute." An so I step out down the street to Barons place bouncin on my heels an tellin my self how I am a big man an let evry body know it.

I get to Barons. Cant tell any thing from the outside. Only one aroun is the super haulin out the cans of garbage. I go up the stairs 3 at a time. Then stop at the door to breath. Then knock. Baron open up.

I say. "Man I sure glad to see you."

He open the door for me an let me in. Miss Dewpont sittin there on the sofa drinkin her cup of coffee. I dont hardly look at her. Baron give me a big smile an shake my hand. "Why Duke." He say. "Now you surely dint think I was goin to stay for ever though I am touched an deeply touched by you kind solictude. Sit down Lad an have a cup of coffee with Miss Dewpont an me."

"Do." Miss Dewpont say. An she go an bring me a cup of coffee.

When she step inta the kitchen Baron say. "Thats one brave girl Lad. Any time I got to be away for a while I know things in good hands." He lean tord me an say. "Uh I hate to mention it like this but if you got rid of the 12."

I hand over the 9 dollas an he tuck it away. He say. "Some un expected legal expenses you know Lad how it is."

Miss Dewpont come in with the cofee. She give me a big smile like this the first time she ever see me. I dont hardly look at her.

Baron put his hand on my leg an say. "Well Lad it can be truly be said that you have been with me thru the good days an the bad. Yes Lad the good days an the bad. The situation a little confused now but we gotta expect that Lad. Thats the way things is in a free economy Lad. You get the fat years an then you get the lean. But it wont be long Lad it wont be long."

I say. "I wasnt worried Royal. I knew they couldnt keep a man like you."

He laugh. He light up a cigar an lean back in his chair. He take the cigar out of his mouth an look at it like he aint seen it befor. "Nothin like the first cigar of the day Lad. Yes." He say. "Yes in a society like ours based as it is on the free enterprise system you gotta expect change. You get a cool period an evrything good. Then you got a confused period like now an evrything aint so good. Some people subscribe

189

to the spots on the sun but I dont know that I subscribe."

I say. "Yeh. Thats right Royal."

"Roy know a thing or 2." Miss Dewpont say to me. She noddin her head like she know whut he talkin about. "Mister Baron an educated man."

Baron take the cigar out of his mouth. He say. "Now I will say this for my former masters an fella subjects of the queen. I will say this. They more serious about education than are we Americans. I will say that. Now you ask me whut about free enterprize? Whut about free enterprize? I was talken about this subjeck not many days ago to a friend of mine who live downtown. An I said to him. Charlie I dont believe for one second free enterprise the end of it an nothing beyond it. But Charlie I tell him. Charlie I will say this. Free enterprize whut we got right now an free enterprize gonna be with us for a while yet to come. So whut I say is. Let us work with it. Let us work with it an within it because it all we got."

I sit there an when he look at me I nod. Royal a smart man I dont care where he come from.

He say to me. "It the ups & downs Lad. It the ups & down of the system. We jus got to lie cool for a while an take it easy."

"It the ony thing to do." Miss Dewpont say noddin her head.

"When the heat off." Baron say. "We move right back in again. Nothin lost for good when you run a tight shop Lad. Cool off for a few weeks an then Poinciana Products be jus as big as they ever once were."

"How long you think it gonna be Royal?" I ask him. "Maybe a day or 2?"

He say. "No Lad. It goin to be more like a week or 2 or maybe even a month."

"Well uh Royal." I say. "Well uh maybe I could jus carry the stuff an keep it inside my gang an no body on the out side know any thing about it."

He take out his cigar an lean tord me. "Lad." He say. "Lad. Lissen to me for I speak to you as would you own Father. Now the time to be cool. Walk out of here with the stuff on you an they got you. They waitin an watchin. I cant do a thing Lad. My hands is tyed. Evry step I make these days is on advice of council."

"Roy." I say. "Jus give me the stuff. I take the responsibility on my self."

"I admire the Lads courage." Miss Dewpont say.

"I admire you courage too Duke." Royal say. An he say to Miss Dewpont. "You right to admire it Miss

Dewpont. But Lad I cant let you have it." He put down his cigar. "The fack is Lad I dont have a single product in the house. You understand Lad. Things bein the way how they are I could not put my self in the position of bein foun here with the supplies. I dont have to spell it out for you Son now do I?"

It all goin. I see it all goin. I think about all the work I put in. I think about all those pennies I spent all my life on jawbreakers an crap like that. Then I stan up an say to my self. "What the hell Man. You cant make it one way you can make it an other."

Royal say. "Duke I promise you that when things cool off again I get word to you right away. We gonna make a whole new deal. I appreciate all you done for the organization an I never forget it."

I ask him if he could let me have 5 till I start workin again. He say he like to. He say they aint nothin he like to do more than lend me 5. But legal expense have took evry penny he could lay his hands on. I say ok an I leave. He take a Ball Point pen off his desk. He say. "Duke as a token of my esteem I like you to have one of my Ball Point pens." I let him clip it on my pocket. I dont tell him he already give me one.

He put his hand on my shoulder an he say. "Duke we got a lot of long years ahead of us. This jus a temporary set back. You know that dont you Lad?"

I say sure I know it. An I leave. Man I feelin real down cast. All I want to do is run over to the Club House an sit down at the table with the gang. Time like this you know whut havin a gang to belong to really mean. It mean you got a place to go to an guys whut care if somethin bad happen to you. It a place where you can go when you in trouble an not jus get kicked at an yell at.

I start out for the club walkin fast an feelin the sweat under my shirt from the heat. The sun poundin down on the street Man an the street givin it right back. So hot it hurt to breath it in. I get half way to the Club house an then I decide. "Why not go up an see Priest an put it on the line with him? Tell him the score an give him the 3 dollars more that I have an savin the 2 for ammo. You never can tell. Maybe he give you the piece." I tell my self.

So I turn aroun an head for Priests place. I run the lass 2 blocks an I feel time rushin pass me an Saturday comin down on me. An me with out the piece. Goin down on them motheren wolves with nothin in my hand but a blade like evry other kid when whut I want an whut I need is to go down burnin.

I run up the stairs 3 at a time. I go up the 4 sets of stairs to the 4th floor an knock on Priests door. An I knock again. I think I can hear some one breathin on

193

the other side the door but no one open the door. I stan an wait. I hold my breath an put my ear against the door. I almos sure I can hear some one jus standen an breathin on the other side of the door. I wait an finely I leave.

I decide no one there. An when I get down an I am standen on the stoop I decide it wouldnt matter even if Priest was there. Priest aint the kind of man to part with somethin without he has the bread in his hand. I could talk for 1 million year an not melt the heart of Priest.

So that leave ony 1 thing to do. Go see Chester.

Down town to Chester

I figure well it gonna cost me 30¢ but it worth it.
Worth the try. If Chester got the bread he give it to
me an if he dont well the 30¢ wont make any big
diffrence the way things are now. So I buy 2 tokens
an I take the Lex down to 77 Street.

The subway hottern the street. People all sittin
there tryin to breath. Some fan themselves with news
papers an others puttin they heads back an restin they
heads on the windas. A man get up an open the door
at the end of the train but all it do is let in a hot wind
that blow all the dirt aroun. Subway not only hottern
the street. It dirtier.

All the men in the subway ridin in the subway they
got super faces. They look like men whut live they
lives rasslin garbage cans an livin in cellars. They
got faces whut look like the faces done as hard work

as they hands. All tired out an wrinkled an beat you know like all you have to do is ask them an they give you evry thing they got. They ready to give it all up any time you ask them loud enough.

When I get out at 77 Street an walk to the apartment house where Chester livin they trees along side the payment an it cooler. The East 70s cooler than whut it is up town. They a lot of these guys in that part of down town in black pants an white sport shirts walken they dogs.

I dont even bother with the uniform man at the door this time. I go aroun where it say SERVICE ENTRANCE and go down inta the cellar. Negro man sittin there readin a news paper at the elevator door. You go down in a cellar any place in this city an you find a Negro man look just like this one readin a news paper.

He say. "Where you come from boy? Dont tell me the drug store finely hire a Negro."

"I dont work for any drug store." I tell him. "I come to see my friend Chester."

He say. "Oh." An fold up the news paper.

I get in the elevator.

He close the door an say. "I guess you must be an old friend of Chesters."

"Thats right." I tell him.

He start the elevator goin. He say. "I could tell

you an *old* friend. You dont look like any of his *new* friends."

"You know if Chester home now?" I ask him.

"Chester always home." He say.

He take me all the way up to the 23 floor. Then he point to a gray door an say. "Go thru that door an turn left. Look for number 237. That Chesters apartment."

I like the sound of that number. 237. It mean luck. I just know it. I find the door an knock. A delivry boy come down the hall an look at me. I knock again. Finely the door open.

"Duke!" Chester say. He real glad to see me. "Man I thought you forgot all about me an give me up for dead. Come on in."

I go in. Chester lookin good. He skinny still but he aint hungry lookin like he uset to be when he livin in hall ways. Chester got a white mans face with a black skin over it. He wearin a white sport shirt with a little aligador sewed on to it an black pants. He wearen on his feet straw slippers with out no backs to them.

"Man I sure am glad to see you. Take a seat an I make you a drink. How bout a martini?" He say.

"Ok." I say. We in the parlor. All the furniture bran new. They a black sofa with a lot of little cushions on it all diffrent colors. An they chairs with wood seats all curved an iron legs look like a bug. Got these crazy paintings hangin on the wall an maybe 100-150 books.

Chester stirrin this drink in a pitcher with ice in it. Must be gin because it dont have any color to it at all. He askin all about the old gang. Most of the guys he askin about have move away or they in correction. Two dead from knife wounds not countin Little Man.

Chester pour out the drinks into these kind of glasses that have a long thin thing at the bottom. They nothin in it but glass. Chester say. "Look like you an me the only ones left Duke Old Man. Lets drink to us."

I take a sip. It pretty good.

"You like it?" He ask me.

I tell him yeh it real good. He say. "Charles says no one can mix a martini as good as me."

"That the guy you livin with Chester? Whut he do for a livin?"

"He runs a employmint agency. Gets people jobs. Hes all right. I really shouldnt complain." He say.

"Whuts a matter with him?"

Chester dont say nothin. Then he say. "Well he dont like to go out with me any wheres. Some times we go out to a movie. But most of the time I just cooped up here like bein in jail."

He pour him self another one of those drinks from the pitcher. "How things with you Duke?" He ask me.

I tell him I now President of the Crocadiles. He say. "Oh Man. Is that kick still on?"

"We pretty strong now Chester."

"Have another drink." He say an pour one for me an for him self. He empty the pitcher into his glass an start mixin some more. "That jazz all seem so far away an long ago to little old me." He say. He sorta half layin on the sofa with his legs cross an some of those cushions under his head. He wave his hands aroun now when he talk. "I comin a long way since those days Duke." He say. "It seem like I a whole diffrent person then in those days. You know whut Duke? I aint been hungry once in the pass 2 years. That the truth Duke. Since the night Charles brought me here I aint been hungry once. No. Hunh uh. I shouldnt ought to complain."

He has to sit up to pour him self another drink but he can drink it layin down. He lay down again. "An look at these close Duke. These pants cost $29.75. This an $8 shirt I wearin. Thats the truth Duke. An you ought to see my winter ward robe. I got a whole closet full in there. I got one pair of pants that is made out of velvet. Two suits an 2 sport jackets with side vents." He sit up an fill his own glass again. He look at me holdin up the pitcher an he say. "Ready for another ducks?"

"Not yet." I tell him.

He run his fingers acrost his for head an say. "Oh dear. Some days you know I jus finish up one of these pitchers all by my self. Well it so *boring*. It such a *bore* jus sittin aroun all day waitin for Charles to come home. They jus so much work I can do aroun here an then they nothin to do but wait. I mean this the kind of digs Man that jus take care of it self."

"I been pretty busy my self Chester."

"Yes ducks I sure you have. Seem like evry body in this whole crazy mix up world have some thing to do except yous truly. Freddy say he really genuinely sorry for me."

"Who Freddy?"

"Freddy the dearest man. A friend of Charles. Oh Charles some time have a party now an again. It isnt that. I have met all his friends. But we jus dont get out much."

"Where you want to go? You got a real nice place here."

"I know it Duke. An really I shouldnt complain. Charles is a dear. But it like Freddy say. He is set in his ways. Oh I dont know." Chester say an he put his hand up to his for head. "I dont know. I just like to pack up an go some wheres. Palm Beech or Vara Derro. Freddy say they wonderful mad places."

"Yeh I been pretty busy with the Club." I say. "An other things." Tryin to get aroun to Priest an the piece an the bread.

Chester puttin the martini away one after an other. He fill his glass an lay down again. "Freddy say I should have all that. He say I the kind who should have evrything my heart desires. But I dont know. Whut do you think Duke?"

"Well it hard to say Chester." I say. "Uh lissen Ches."

He say. "You let me know when it get close to 5 oclock Duke. Charles come home then an get insane jealous if he find you here. That an other thing. He go wild when he see me jus *lookin* at some body else." Chester flip his hand over on the cushion. He got long fingers an his finger nails shine like they got polish on them. But they aint polisht. They got natural color.

"Some times I get so bored I could cry." Chester say sippin the martini. "Honest to GOD Duke I swear some times I wish I was back up town hungry an misrable an with out a roof over my head. But then when it rain or when it cold out I remember how it uset to be an how I uset to wrap news papers aroun my legs an scrounge for food. When I remember it times like that I could jus kiss the groun that Charles walk on for takin me out of all that. Oh the stink an the misry Duke I jus cant go back to it no matter how bad things is here."

"You doin all right here Chester." I tell him.

"Did I tell you Duke I got 2 suits an 2 sport jackets with side vents?" He ask me.

"Yeh you told me Chester." I say.

"Side vents is those slits on the side." He say. "An I got a winter coat oh Man you oughta see it. So soft an warm. It got a all packa linin like fur you know."

"Yeh." I say. "Uh lissen Ches. Priest has a Colt thats goin for 15 an I got 5 down on it an I wonderin if you could lend me 10 so I could pick it up for Saturday night." I finely say it.

Chester face get all mad. He sit up. "Now this is just the lass straw." He say.

"Oh it ok if you dont have it Chester." I say thinkin he mad at me because the only reason I finely come to see him is to ask for the lend of money.

"It the lass straw." He say sittin up an his martini stuff sloshin aroun in the glass. "No pin money. Not a penny of pin money does he give me because he scared I walk out on him. Freddy say he never heard of such a thing an that I should have all that my heart

202

desire. An now when a friend the oldest friend I got in this crazy world come to me for the loan of 10 I cant give it to him."

"Hell Man." I say. "It ok. I make out some how Ches."

"I cant reach into my pocket an take out the 10 an say. Friend. Old friend. Here you are an I sorry I cant do better."

"Why sure Ches. I knowed you would do it if you could. Dont get all up set on my account Ches."

"Up set?" He say. "Up set. You bet I up set. You dont know whut I do for that man an whut I put up with an him so set in his way as Freddy says." He pour him self some more of the martini an begin to drink it. "Oh Christ." He say. "I bein too selfish ducks. Here." An he pour whut left in the pitcher inta my glass. Tears rollin down his face. He shake his head an bite his lip. "Oh dear I am sorry. Charles say I am a spoiled darlin an I guess that whut I am. Goin on like this an thinkin ony of my self. Whut must you think of me Duke Man?"

"Well you makin out all right Ches. Look like you got a nice deal here." I say.

"Oh materal things aint evry thing Duke. I can tell you that Man from the bottom of my heart. I up to here with materal things but when it come to pin money not a penny do I get." An he start cryin again.

I sit there in one of those chairs that like a bug an wondrin why did I ever come. Time slippin away. Maybe Priest home now. An the 30¢ I spendin for subways.

He say. "Life ought to be good ducks but it so motheren awful." An he cry holdin the empty glass in his hand. He forget he holdin it.

Chester sigh a big shuddering sigh an he stop cryen an smile at me. "Oh dear." He say. "I do feel better now. I always feel better for a good cry. No Duke I shouldnt complain. Dont get the idee that I aint satisfied with my luck. I got evry thing here." He wave his hand aroun. He pick up a little green statue from the table. "I jus love jade things dont you? An if it dont work out you know with Charles why they are others who want me. They are quite a few whut want me Duke. I could jus pack my bag right this minute an move in to any one of 3 places. Not only Freddy who is always after me an always promisin. Trips to Palm Beech an Verra Derro an other beautiful places. But Jim Andersen I notice he lookin at me in a certain way an they is one other whose name I will not mention. Not that youd know him ducks it jus that I have the feelin it would be bad luck to say his name out loud."

"Yeh." I say. "Well you got to watch out all the time for bad luck Ches. It can kill you."

"Well I dont know ducks." He say like he real tired. "I dont know. It aint like up town. Down here you dont die of it. It jus make you a little un happy." He say. "Duke I hate to mention it but Charles will be gettin back soon."

I stand up right away. I have to get movin. It a bad day all aroun an nothin gettin done that have to get done. But before he leave me go he take me in the bed room an show me his 2 suits an his 2 sport jackets an the winter coat. It all nice stuff. An a draw full of shirts of all kinds. Finely we finished an Ches walk me out to the service elevator an ring the bell.

When the elevator come an the old man open the door Ches say. "Take care of you self ducks."

I tell him to take care of him self too an then the door close an I ride down 23 floors to the cellar with the old man. He dont say nothin to me an I dont say nothin to him.

Rockets & outerspace & things like that

I made it back to the Lex subway an jus in time for the rush. Train jammed to the doors with sweatin people comin home from work. It make me laugh inside to look at them. All of them so beat an worryed an knocked out. They so tired lookin you could take any thing from them you wanted. Some of them all scrunched up in the cars tryen to read they news-papers.

I standen next to a PR readen a news paper written in Porto Rican. Front page have a picture of some dead people layin on the floor of a room an some big print in Porto Rican I guess it tellin you that they dead. I standen right up front in the first car up against the door so I can see the tunnel an far down the track you can see the stations comin tord you.

I like it up there in front. You get the feelin that

you rushin thru the tunnel like a jet. Whooom! You put you head right up against the glass so you cant see nothin of the train an then you get the feelin they is nothin aroun you or under you but only speed. Come roarin thru an when I see the station comin I step down soft on the brake an bring it to a stop. Smooth Man.

When I was a kid I uset to like to do that when I go down town shoppin with my Mother. I stan at the door with my nose against the glass an pretend I the driver. Kids get they kicks easy.

I think to my self Man if only this was a rocket an me at the controls. Voooom! An I headin for outer space an point her nose tord the moon. I talk into my head piece an I say to the crew. "All right you guys now settle down back there an lissen to this. Our barins is nawt nawt 2 an we goin east by west. I want you to check all them ailerons an send me up a cup of coffee."

An Man we Go! Passin stars an comets an things like that. Jus roarin thru outerspace at a 100 miles a second. Or maybe more. Nothin up there but stars an a deep blue a deep blueness an the moon maybe a 1 million miles straight ahead an we goin straight for it. It comin up big an silver on my screen like a TV set where I watch where I goin.

The sun is over on the left an I wearen special made glasses so it dont blind me if I come too close because of the glare. The boy come up with the coffee an I set my controls on the auto matic control an sit back an drink my coffee. Sit there an watch the screen to see whut doin in outerspace.

Moon an stars. Moon an stars thats all they is out in outerspace. I switch on the sound to see what I can hear. Wind. Wind an my rocket engins roarin. Thats the only sound. It so clean an pure in outer space it kill you like that if you take one breath. Thats whut they say. I read it in a science comic book. When you go out of the rocket ship you got to wear a bubbel on you head so you dont have to breath that poison air.

I take a look at my barins an see we in the moons orbit at lass. I tell my men. "Ok fellas we goin in." Then I pull back on the thing an swing us aroun an set us down easy on our tail. When you land a rocket ship whut you gotta do is you gotta reverse the engins.

Oh Man. I look aroun me. Lot a times on the subway I see people talken out loud. But no body looken at me. The PR standen next to me still readin his Porto Rico news paper. He shaken his head at whut he readin. He say. "I.I.I.I." Like that. "I.I.I.I." Shakin his head alla time

"Oh new ayva york." He say. "Oh new ayva york. I. I. I." New ayva york is PR for New York. They a lot a people on the subway always talken to they selfs. You see them on the streets too. But mostly on the subways because they think other people cant hear them whut they sayin.

Rumble is on

We got hold of Foxys friend this kid who livin in Wolve territory an that way we set up a Meet between the 2 Prime Minsters. Cowboy an the Wolves Prime Minster hold they Meet in a lunchenette in neutral turf. I tell Cowboy whut to tell him. This other guys name is Little Flower an Cowboy say he dont know about the others but Little Flower aint on the junk.

Cowboy has the Meet with him an tells him whut I told him. That we aint the kind of gang whut makes raids. We lettin them know. Saturday night is the night. We comin down on they turf an evry thing goes.

Little Flower say. "Well ok Man. We thought you was all dead or gone social the way we dint hear from you after we japped that friend of your."

Cowboy say to him. "We choosin our own time

Man. We dont jump cause the Wolves say jump."

"An then after Little Man we still dont hear from you Man why we think the Crocadiles not boppin no more." Little Flower say. "Man you shoulda hear the things guys sayin about you."

Cowboy tell him we dont care whut Wolves say about us.

Little Flower say. "Angel sayin that Crocadiles eat shit."

Cowboy give him a big smile an look him up an down you know. Real cool. Then he stand up slow an easy. "We be seein you. Saturday night Man."

"We be waitin for you." Little Flower say.

Then Cowboy come back to the Club House an tell us whut happen at the Meet. The guys get mad when they hear whut the Wolves been sayin. "Them motherens." They say. An. "Man they wont talk so big when we get thru with them."

Saint say. "We be ready for them. We ready for them." An he take out his tablet an make an other count again. Saint give me a report on the blade situation an we still runnin short. Rod say. "Uh huh it always that way. Guys afraid they gonna lose a good blade. You see Duke half of em gonna turn up with bread knifes."

"A bread knife can do the job." Saint say.

"Aint no doubt of that in the world." Rod say. "A bread knife will do the job. We all know that."

"But that aint whut a bread knife made for." Cowboy say to Saint. "That whut Rod mean. Oh it can do the job it can do the job Man. But so can a brick. You put a man out with a bread knife why Man you jus dont have style with it."

"It dont look good." Rod say.

Saint tell them. "Man I know it dont look good but whut can I do? I have done all I can an they still some Crocadiles whut will have to go down with kitchen knifes."

I say. "The Wolves prolly gonna have plenty of guys arm with the same thing. That gang fallin apart. Angel on junk we know that for sure. An then all that time Blood aroun keepin us down why dint the Wolves jump us then? They knew we was weak an dint have no leader ship. It because they weak too."

Cowboy say. "I agree with you Man. I think Angel gonna have to do some fass husslin to round up 50 men."

Bishop came in from Little Mans room holdin a zip gun an he say to Saint. "Saint show me how to load up this piece." Saint give him Little Mans piece the one he made in shop right under Mister Swenlunds nose.

Saint say. "Man these new men learn slow." An he get up an take Bishop inta Little Mans room because that the Armory now.

Cowboy say. "I think Saturday night gonna be the end of the Wolves. Little Flower talk tough but he look scared."

I tell Cowboy an Rod. "You guys take over here for a little while. I gonna run over an see Priest."

"How you makin out about that bisness?" Rod say.

I say. "I think I be able to get it from Priest. I got 5 down with him an if I give him 3 more why I think he let me have it."

"I dont know." Cowboy say.

"You gonna have to do some real talkin to get it out of Priest." Rod tell me. "Man if you need some bread you know I be glad to raise it for you."

"I like to make it my self Rod."

"It better to make it you self." Cowboy say. "It good luck for the piece when you make it you self."

"Yeh." I say. "Well you know Rod if I have to have it why I come to you." An I stan up an look aroun gettin ready to go. That when we hear the bang. From the Armory. An evry body get quiet an dont move.

Saint come to the door. He say. "The god dam zip went off. The bullet in the wall."

Bishop say. "It just went off in my motheren hand Duke."

I tell them all to shut up an not make a soun. I pinch out the candel an we all sit an stand there just like the bang found us. The whole house quiet. Evry body in that house hear that shot an evry body sittin in they own apartment quiet an waitin. We wait five or maybe 10 minute an nothin happen. No one knock on the door. Cops dont come. I say to Cowboy. "Leave it dark an keep quiet. I goin now." An I slip out the door.

Goin down the stairs that bilding like a empty bilding. You never know a 100 people livin there. Evry door is dark an the whole place quiet. No body want any trouble. I go out side an no body on the stoop. I laugh to my self thinkin of all those people sittin in they hot stinkin apartments without no lights on jus because Bishop got a nervus finger.

I went on up to Priests. I went up those stairs so quiet if any body listenin behind the door they never know. I stan at the door an not breath an just lissen. No sound so quiet I know nothin but a empty apartment behin that door. I knock any way. I knock again an wait. No body. Priest gone. I know it in my bones.

I go down to the first floor an find the super. He

an old man sittin in the kitchen with his wife. She wearin glasses an sewin a patch on his work pants. "You lookin for some body?" The old man ask me.

I tell him I got a message for Priest an ask him do Priest live in this bilding.

He say. "Yes he do an he pay his rent regular an is a quiet livin man. He one tenant I dont have no complaint about. You one of his childern?"

"No I a friend of his an juss passin by an wonderin do Priest still live here?"

"You got the right place all right." The old man say.

"You have any idee when he comin home?" I ask.

"I dont keep track of all them people who livin here. I dont know when the last time I see Priest." He start gettin mad the old man like I keepin him from some thing important you know. That old man aint had nothin important to do for 20 years.

I go on out an I stan on the stoop lookin left & right sort of hopin I see Priest come walkin down the street. But he aint no where that man. I walk aroun the block an when I come to Hermits I go on in.

"Well." He say. "You still alive?"

"You seen Priest lately Hermit?" I ask him.

Hermit laugh. "Now there a popular man that Priest. Two guys come in here yestiday askin me the same question."

I sit down at the counter. "Whut kind of guys?" I ask him.

"Jus guys Duke jus guys. I haven seen Priest for 2-3 days. Whut can I do for you?"

I get a ham sanwich an a coke. Whut the hell. I might as well blow the money on eats. I sit an eat an thinkin in 3 or 4 day now all I eatin is ham sanwiches an hot dogs. I dint mean to leave home but it just happen. You stay away one night an a second night an a third an then it dont seem like it worth goin back an havin to lissen to you Mother yell at you. So I just keep on not goin back.

It easier for me than for Chester now. He got a lot of close to pack an things like that. He got belongins. An like that man Charles he livin with. All that new furniture an those maybe 200 books an things. A man like that cant just pick up an go. But I got the shoes I wearin an maybe 2 more pants an a winter jacket an maybe 4 shirts an thats all. When you like like me it as easy to go as to stay. That why so many go because it so easy.

Hermit open a book an show me a pictcher of a big town with an ocean an a payment with wavy lines in it. I never see any thing like that payment before. He say. "You know whut town that is? That Reeo Janeero in Brazil."

"They got real crazy payments." I say.

"I jus been readin this book all about Brazil." Hermit say. "You know they aint no color line in Brazil? I never knew it my self till the other day a fella came in here an was talkin about it. I got this book from the library."

"Why dont you go down an live in Brazil?" I ask him.

"I do it in a flash Duke if it wasnt for the langwige." Hermit say. "But I too old to learn an other langwige now. They talk Porchageez in Brazil the book say. If I was you age Duke I do it. I do it in a flash. Go down there an live out my days in full equality like GOD intended.

I ask him. "How about that deal with the lumber mill you got goin in Africa?"

"Well it still on the fire Duke. I aint put it out of my mind yet. I still considerin the possibilities Duke."

"How you know GOD intended?" I ask him.

"Whut?" He say.

"How you know GOD intended we to live equals with them?"

"Why Man." He say. "Man it all in the Bibel. Evry body is brothers the Bibel say. Evry body know that."

"Maybe evry body in Brazil know it." I say.

Hermit un tie his apron an tie it again tighter. He say. "Yeh they know it in Brazil an a couple other places."

"It taken a long time for the word to get aroun Hermit."

"Well but we come a long way Duke. We come a long way."

"Oh Man." I say.

"Since they chained us an bound us an pack us like sardines in those ships Duke we come a long way."

I put down the money for the sanwich. I say. "You aint my brother Hermit because you soft in the head." An I walk to the door.

I go walkin back to the Club house laughin inside thinkin about all the slobs I passin on the street that they my brothers. I think about evry bilding I pass an evry door in them got a iron flandge on it to keep they brothers out who want to rob them. Oh Man I think dont talk brother talk to me.

When I get to the house Rod sittin on the stoop waitin for me. He tell me evry body has cleared out an he waitin to see did I get the piece from Priest. I tell him whut happen.

"Duke Man it dont look good." He say.

I stan there kickin the step. That all I feel like doin. "You think he comin back Rod?"

"It dont look that way to me Duke. To me it look like someone lookin for him an he know it an he took off with whut he can carry."

That the way it look to me too.

"Well it only 5 dollars." Rod say.

"It aint the 5." I tell him. "It the piece. I wanted that piece bad Man. I wanted to go down on them Wolves burnin an now I have to go down like evry body else with a blade in my hand mixin it up like a kid."

"I know how it is Duke. Aint nothin like a piece. I held a piece in my hand once made me feel like I own the whole motheren world. But this aint the last chance Man. They be other times. We only jus startin Man. Next rumble come along I know you gonna have you piece."

"Yeh." I say.

He stan up to go. "Well Man." He say.

"You goin home now?" I ask.

"Home." He say. "No I meetin a guy over at the movies. Duke I see you tomorra first thing." He say. "An I keep my eyes open. You never know. Somethin always turnin up Man."

I sit on the stoop an watch him go. If I had some stones I break evry window on the block. Thats how I feel. I know Priest aint ever gone to be there ever

219

again. He gone for good like evry body else who ever gone. They dont come back aint no point comin back. Start some wheres else just as easy or easier.

After a while I start to thinkin about Sue Randolph. I aint thought of her for a long time. I think about goin up to her place but I decide No the hell with it. Then after I sit there a while I walk on back to Priests an lissen at the door an knock an wait. But he gone. So I went back to Little Mans an walk back an forth thru the apartment thinkin about Priest an Sue Randolph and the rumble comin. An I say to my self Man it all fell apart in you hand. You had it made Man an now it all gone. Well I say to my self You knowed it would happen that way an that the way it happen.

Then I remembered the Armory an went inta Little Mans room an opened it. Saint got 3 matchetes we dint have befor. Saint doin a good job. I take out the blades an look them over an finely I pick one for my self. I pick the best one in the Armory. I mean Man if you have to go down with a blade make sure it the best you can get.

We go down

I wake up Saturday morning with a bad hang over from the wine. Have drank too much of that stuff jus sittin there by my self after evry body leave. Nothin else to do. I get up an go in the kitchen an make my self some coffee. I think to my self God dam it here I am makin my self coffee again. Evry day the same an I dont see nothin ahead but the same for me.

I walkin aroun bare foot wearen nothin but shorts. My chest hard as a rock an I got good arms. Hard an strong but not mussel bound like some guys. With them it all for show those Mister America guys you know. Mussels like that aint worth nothin when things get rough.

Waitin for the water to boil. It take a long time on the Sterno. I look aroun that kitchen an say Oh Christ seein the greasy stove an the sink full of roaches. They so many roaches they aint even scared of me. They jus like settin there waiten for me to leave. You kill one an 50 get away.

The floor all rollin an heavin like the ocean at Coney. In them bildings the floor never strait. It either buckle or it tilty. You put down linoleum an all it do is crack. Some time you move into a new place an start takin up the old linolum you find maybe 5 or 6 layers of linoleum. Evry body try to straiten out the floor. You cant no more straiten out the floors than you can get rid of the roaches.

Water drippin in the sink all the time. They always a leak in some thing if it aint the sink it the tub or the toilet. Evry apartment I can remember since I was a kid you can lay in bed an at night when it quiet you can hear a drip from some where.

Apartments make me sad. I get down cast jus walkin inta the hall of the places where I live. I dont want to walk up the stairs to my place. It aint worth it. Lot of guys feel that way. They just as soon stay out in the hall. In the winter time when it cold out side the halls of all these bildings fulla kids. They neck in the halls. Have fights in the halls. Smoke pot in the halls. The halls just as good as inside the apartment. An some times better. Shitman I liven in places like this all my life an you think I woulden know no better. An maybe I dint. All I know is I walk inta the door an see all those mail boxes with they doors ripped off or jimmyed open an hangin there. See the floors an the garbage cans under the stairs makin a stink. An Man I get down cast an I dont want to go up it only get worse.

Finely the water boil an I put in the instant an drink it. I think Man tonight is the night. I think Man you got to get on over to Priests an see if he back yet. An then I say Oh give it up Man give it up. You know he aint comin back. The hell with it. Aint worth it. Forget it. I got no heart for the rumble now. I in it an I aint gonna chicken out but I dont have the heart for it no more. I put the whole gang in it. I set it up. I gonna go thru with it.

But I dont care any more. It all gone bad on me with out I havin the piece. An so I say to my self Man you dont have the piece an may be you aint gone to get the piece but Man you got the gang. You got a place. You a leader. You belong. Lot of guys countin on you.

Man I tell you comes a time they aint nothin to do but whut you have to do. It dont matter like it or not like it. You in it Man an you do it. You gotta swing with the gang. Or you out. You on the street with no protection an all alone.

223

They aint law on the streets. No an none in the houses. You ask me why an I tellin you why we do whut we have to do. Because when they aint law you gotta make law. Other wise evry thing wild Man an you dont belong an you alone. No body want that I dont care who you are a doctor or whut ever you are I dont care. No body want that.

So we go in the gang. We start hangin aroun an become a junior an then we grow up some more an get takin in the gang. Then we belong an we part of the thing an not scared out on the edge.

I get washt an drest finely an finish the wine an finely Foxy come. He never smile that kid. I never see him smile. He got big round eyes always lookin at you with out blinkin.

"Foxy Man I glad you here." I tell him. "Got a few jobs for you." I give him 3 of my dollars. Whut the hell whut else can I do but spend it. "Find Rod." I tell him. "Give him this an tell him to get holt of some more. He know whut it for. Tell him I want the juice for tonight."

Foxy take the money an he hold it in his hand. He make a fist aroun it like a little kid goin to the store. Well an that all he is. A little kid. Next time I notice him he layin on the street with his cheek laid open by a aireal. But he pull thru all right.

In a little while Foxy come back an say. "I foun him. He say he bring the juice."

I take the jug with me an go up front an lay down on the bed. They aint much left in it an I finish it off. Then I go to sleep again. When I wake up a lot of the guys in Little Mans old room pickin they arms up for the rumble an arguin about who gets whut. I dont pay no atention. Rod comin soon with the juice an it all get set right. It dont matter.

I send Foxy down to Hermit to bring me back a couple ham sanwiches. Drinkin on a empty stomach no good you gotta have a linin for it. I eat the sanwiches then an dont talk to no body. Guys come up an ask me questions I just dont look at them. They still time.

Aroun 4 oclock Rod still aint come an I send 2 Snakes out lookin for him an I tell Foxy to go an knock on Priests door see if he back yet. The Snakes dont find Rod. He come in him self an Cowboy with him. They got the stuff.

They take it out of the bags an set it out on the table. They got 3 bottles of liquor an 2 jugs of muscatel. I say. "You guys did real good. We start on this stuff aroun 6 o'clock when it do us the most good."

Rod say. "Duke Man I thought this night never

come. I thought if it dont come soon I gonna bust wide open. Man the cool been on too long. I got a lot in me to get rid of Man. Man I gonna un load on them Wolves tonight."

"Whuts the plan Duke?" Cowboy say.

I lean back in my chair. I say. "I been thinkin about that. An they aint no plan. We just go in wild."

"Thats the best way." Rod say. "That the best way Man. No body ever folla the plan any way. When the thing start it all go wild evry time."

Foxy come back an he shake his head. I knew it all the time. I wasnt expectin any thing else. Well I say to my self whut the hell. Go down with the knife like evry body else doin. It aint 6 yet but I say. "Lets get started." An Rod an Cowboy open the bottles an the wine an we start drinkin.

The guys all so keyed up it dont take long maybe two drinks befor they start feelin it. The place all filled up. Some guys I never see befor even. The hell with it if they want to swing with us tonight it they own funral. Saint walkin aroun with his tablet checkin evry body out makin sure evry body got arms. Saint doin a good job. He can take responsibilty.

Guys sittin on the floor an standen. Some of them in Little Mans old room. The bottles go down the line out of the kitchen inta Little Mans room an back again. Evry body take a big swalla of the wine an a little nick of the liquor. That the best way to do it. Couple of the kids get sick an throw up in the toilet. That always happen. Soon as they come out we give them a shot of the liquor to fix them up.

Some guys settin in the corner near the door passin a little bottle of they own. They aint drinkin it but only breathin it. Hold it up to they nose an taken deep breaths. I walk over to them an see whut it is. Cherokee one of them. He say. "Duke Man this is the stuff." He hold it up to his nose an breath it in. "Man!" He say.

"Whut you got there?" I ask him. An he hand me the bottle. Cleanin fluid is whut it is. Cherokee say. "Man it the new thing. Wild. Crazy Man. It got a kick." I take a deep breath of it. Man it stink some thin awful. I hand it back to Cherokee. "I glad you guys gettin a charge out of it." I say. An they all laugh crazy laughs. They the kind of guys some one tell them you can get high on this stuff why they get high on it. Tell them water make them high they get high on water.

I go back to the table. "How you feelin Rod?" I say.

"Gettin there Man. I gettin there." He say.

Cowboy say. "Oh Man." An pass me the bottle.

"You forgettin somethin Duke." Rod say.

I look at him an try to think whut I am forgettin. Finely I ask him whut I forgettin.

"Whut you promise to call me." He say.

"Oh yeh." I say. "That right."

"Whuts that?" Cowboy say.

"Rods new name. Black Death. That his new name."

Cowboy say. "I like it. I like it."

About 30 guys in the kitchen now an some more in Little Mans room. The aireals wavin an some got the cutlasses an matchetes acrost they laps. Evry body drinkin an talken it up about whut they gonna do to the Wolves. Them motherens. We gonna kill them motherens. I keepin a sharp eye out. Because once I in on a rumble in the old days when I was a kid first in the gang an evry body got so drunk an fulla hate we start fightin each other. You got to watch them all the time.

When the bottles come back to us I hold them on the table for a while befor I start passin them again. Most of the guys are takin it all right but some are just leanin on the walls an laughin they heads off.

"I gettin there." Rod say. "I gettin there slow an sure Man."

"We all gettin there." Cowboy say. He rub his

chest after evry swalla he take. "Oh Man." He say.
"Oh Man them motheren Wolves. I gonna pick out a
man an cut him in half."

"Them motherens." Rod say. "Before we through
they gonna know why my name whut it is." An he
make a thrust. He put the twist on it. "Tonight." He
say. "An no mistake. I mean it Man I mean it. I
mean it. Tonight some one gonna get it an they
gonna get it from me. Duke Man aint it time yet?
Gettin dark."

"It always dark in here." I say. "Theys time." I
start passin the bottles again. This is the last round.
When it over we go. We move out. I keep a bottle
between my legs an share it with Cowboy an Rod. It
burn me like my insides raw. I feel my lips gettin like
numb. That the way it always happen with me. Then
it like freeze up aroun my eyes.

The bottles goin from hand to hand movin in an
out among the aireals that swayin back an forth acrost
the kitchen. I feel like clickin noises in my head an
swayin back an forth in my chair. I know it time now
but I dont move. I sit an sway back an forth like I
tryin to make it up. But I aint even tryin.

Rod say. "Man it time Man it time. Lets go Man
lets go." An all the guys start. "It time Man. Lets
go lets go lets go."

Then I standen up an I dont even know how I got standen up. Rod on his feet too an the whole room movin. "We movin out." I say. "Now not too many at once. An keep you arms hidden. Dont get pick up by the cops befor you even get where we goin." They start movin out. I send Rod out after the first bunch an then Cowboy go with the second. I look aroun for Saint an give him the sign to go with the last bunch. The door still open. I alone. I touch the blade under my shirt an step out closin the door behin me.

On the street I see the guys movin. They spread out on both payments an headin east. We movin. From the stoop I see Rod leadin the first bunch across the street an turnin tord downtown. Cowboy takes his bunch a block more an Saint take his men aroun the other side. When we all set we move in from 3 sides move in on them where they waiten.

They waiten in the play ground at the projeck. A big place with a black tar ground an white painted lines on it for hop scotch an games like that for kids. An swing an sliding boards and like that. It cut off from the street by the cars parked along side it.

The Wolves waiten. A lot of them I dont know how many. I see Angel an maybe 10 guys with him standen by the sand box. I reach in my shirt for the blade. My skin cold an I can feel my heart poundin in there.

Cowboy an Rod give the wistle an I tap Saint on the shoulder. "We go." I say. An we runnin in tord them an I see Cowboy an Rod an they men movin in an some Wolves facin us an some turn to face the others.

Then we mixin with them in among them an I hear the swipe an swish of the aireals an guys sayen. "Oh you motheren. Oh you motheren. Oh you motherens. I kill you motheren bastards." An I keep my left arm up for protection an my back all hunched over. I dont see Angel any where. I looken for him. I movin aroun an lookin. I see Foxy layin they with his face laid open. An some guys I dont know weather they Wolves or Crocadiles jus sittin on the ground with the blood runnin down they faces.

"Custis! Duke Custis! I lookin for you." I hear Angel. An then I see him. He standen on top of the sliden bord laughin an lookin at me. The first zip gun go off right behin my head an I drop. They shooten at Angel. He just stand there an laugh at them an call my name.

I try to get to him. A Wolf tangle with me an I get him in the shoulder. I see the blood spread on his shirt. "You motheren Crocadile." He say an I bang his head on the ground. Then the Wolves start burnin. One of them got a piece He fire 2 times an I guess that all the ammo he have. I look up jus in time to see

Cowboy goin down. He fall flat on his face the back of his head all shot away.

I hear the sirens then an the cop wistles start. Evry body start to run. Those that can run. Rod an I make it to the sliding bord together. He musta lost his blade. I see him pick up some bodys bread knife they have dropped. Angel jump an take off runnin. He fast Man. I seen him do it befor. Rod an I take out after him.

We folla him. We follad him between the projeck bildings an tare after him thru bushes an aroun parked cars. The projeck guard step out in front of us but when he see the blade he step out of the way. When we get past him he start blowin his wistle.

Angel headin for the river first an then he turns. He lost on the turn. I dont know why he done it. He shoulda know better than that. Rod right behin him an I watchin Rods legs not to trip him up. Oh Man I say to my self. Oh Man where my blade? Because while I running suddenly I relize I musta drop my blade some where.

Then we come to a place along side one of the bild- ings they high green bushes growin with little red berrys on them. It was right there that Angel stumbeld an he moan when he hit the groun. He half way up when Rod on him an they go twistin inta the bushes both of them makin cryin noises from they mouths. I go in after them an Rod got his left arm aroun Angels neck an they rockin an pullin against each other an then Rod put on the pressure. An for a second they still. An they strain against each other. An Rod push the bread knife into Angels back.

I see Angels face. He closen his eyes real tight. He press them closed an his mouth pull up. He fall down front wards an lay without movin talken in Porto Rican. "Sue cio." He say. "Sue cio. Sue cio. Sue cio."

Then he start moanin. An Rod say. "I tol you I do it an I do it." Angel moanin. Rod lookin at me. Then he bend down an pull the blade out. Angel say. "Thank you." An we left him an took off tord the river.

I get picked up

We left him dead with his face turn side ways an his hair all muss up. The cops wistles all aroun us an we can hear them runnin they feet poundin the payments thru the projeck. Lights goin on in the windas an the bildings loomin up aroun us. We stay in side the bushes an head tord the river again.

"We better seprate." Rod say.

"Go ahead." I tell him.

He say. "I get rid of the blade." Then he disapeer sayin. "See you aroun Duke." I can jus barely see him then in the shadas of the bilding movin fast. No one else coulda seen him.

I sat there in the bushes a little while with my head restin on my knees. I so awful motheren tired I dont think I can stand up but I know I got to get out of that place an away Man. So finely I push off an snake outa there stayn in the shadas of the bildings an crawlin in the bushes an between the park cars. I hear the cops wistlin an I seen the wagon go by an a ambulance come. I went in the cellar of one of the bildings an walked thru an come out the other side. Finely I make it out an walk under the east river drive where it dark. I walk up town a long ways befor I turn an go across town. About 25 blocks an then when I get to my street I have 25 more to walk goin down town.

It only about 10 oclock or 10 30. I thinkin it should be early in the mornin by now. An I look aroun like wonderin what all these people doin on the street why aint they home in bed. They all Porto Ricans an the record store got loud speakers over the doors playin Porto Rican music. People walkin up an down talkin an laughin. People standen on corners talk an laughin.

I want to say to them. "Stop laughin I could stop you laughin if I told you. You Angel dead an layn in the bushes down at the projeck." Then they stop laughin.

Man but I too tired to talk to any body. I jus draggin my body down the street 25 blocks. I countin the streets. 24. 23. 22. Like that. I make it at lass. I walk up the stoop. No body there an I glad of that. Summer nights usely Mister Hurst settin out there smokin his pipe. I get to the bottom of the stairs an look up. Man I cant do it. I too tired to have to lissen to my Mother yellin at me an tellin me her troubles. In stead I go down the hall to where the garbage cans is under the stairs an I crawl under the stairs where the stairs almost touchin the floor an I lay down an go to sleep. I fall right asleep I so tired.

I dont know how long I been sleepin there when I wake up an see Mister Hurst lookin down at me. I look up at him an he look down at me. He dont say nothin. I crawl out an stand up. My legs feel all funny an I guess I start to go down. He take holt of my arm an walk me down the hall an we go inta his apartment.

He sit me in the big chair facin the TV an make me coffee. He dont say a word till he bring me the coffee. Then he sit down on a wood chair an say. "Was it you done the killin Richard?"

I too tired to talk. I just shake my head No. I drink the coffee. He fill his pipe an light it an puff away at it for a while. He so big he make that chair he sittin in look like a kids chair in school. He look like bullets an knifes just bounce off him like off a stone wall. Finely he say. "I sit here thinkin what to say to you Richard an they aint nothin I have to say to you." He look at me. "You know whut gone to happen now dont you?" He ask me.

I say. "Yeh I know." He nod his head. I say.

"But maybe they wont find me. Maybe they dont even know where to look."

He dont say nothin. We sit there for a while an no body say any thing. He get up an turn on a little radio he got on a shelf. He switch the dial aroun lookin for a news report. I hear the announcer talkin about the news. Trouble evry where all over the world. Then he say. "Here in New York." An he talk about the rumble an how a boy got killed. When I hear it it dont sound like it have any thing to do with me.

Mister Hurst say. "How it happen? God dam it how it happen to you boys? It never uset to be as bad as this. They too many people." He say. "They too many people now that whut the trouble is. So many people in this city that the people like an ocean an you can drown in it an no body ever notice."

I fall asleep again an when I wake up I dont know whut time it was when I wake up the radio still playin an Mister Hurst still sittin in that chair smokin his pipe. Man on the radio talkin about the fall out an how it poisonin the air. Then they a knock on the door an Mister Hurst say. "Come in." That voice of his go right thru 10 doors.

That where they picked me up. My Mother with them. They musta gone up to our apartment first an then they come to Mister Hursts. One of them come over to me an say. "Get up. On you feet kid." I try to get up but I cant. Me legs give out on me. I cant feel them like. He take my arm an pull me up. "Come on. Come on." He say. I fall right over on my face. My Mother scream.

They pick me up one each side an start to drag me out. The tips of my shoes hissin on the linoleum an then when we get out in the hall where the linoleum in little squares my shoes go thic thic thic thic thic all the way down the hall. An I hear my Mother screamin an cryn an sayin all the time. "I give him up. I give him up. I give him up. I give him up."

They throw me on the floor in the back of the police car. One of them get in the back with me. He sit on the seat. He put his two feet on me where I layin on the floor. I sayin to myself It aint me. It aint me. I two people an this one aint me.

Where I am

I in this place now where they send me. In the country up in New York State. We got trees an flowers an like that. We got seasons. Right now it winter. Befor it was fall. I live in like a real house. About 10 other guys livin there. Mister Henderson an his wife they live in the house too. We got a baseball dimond an they other houses like this one an a big bilding where they teach us things like shop an school classes. One day a week I stop in at the docs office an we talk about things.

The judge say. "I dont care if they aint room for him. You make room hear? I aint sendin him back to the streets. You find a bed. I aint sendin him back." The judge he was all rile up. The court room full of Crocadiles an Wolves an cryn Mothers. My Mother cryn with the rest of them. I try not to look at her but I always turnin aroun to see if she still in the room. It was over in 3-4 days an then after a couple more days the Youth people brought me here.

Doc Levine say I doin real good. He give me the flower beds to tend because I like that kind of work. It the first kinda work I ever really done. An I doin good in the school classes. I learnin how to spell an write an I can read real good now.

The other guys is ok. Some of them all they think about is gettin back with the gangs again. They dont like it here. I got a friend name Ramon. Thats Raymond in Porto Rican. We in the same room an some days he help me with the flowers even though it not his job. He takin up carpentery.

One day he workin with me in the flower beds. I puttin down peat moss aroun the rose bushes to keep them good thru the winter. I say to him. "Hey Ramon what do sue cio mean in Porto Rican."

"Whut word?" He say.

"Sue cio."

"Oh." He say. "It mean dirty. Filthy. Why you wanta know?"

"No reason." I say.

They this little town near by where they got houses made out of bords an painted white an green. They got a movie. One movie in the whole town that how little that place is. Some times Mister Henderson an his wife take us in to see a movie.

Doc Levine makin an arrangement with the school in that town. Next year a few of us gone to be allowed to go to school in town with the town kids. Doc say if I keep on like I am maybe I can go. Once you know how to read it aint hard to learn almos any thing. Doc say. "Readin. To read Richard. That the beginnin of evry thing. You see if I not right Richard. Man." He say. "When you can read an write why you can do any thing. Do any thing. Be any thing."

Some times I think about the old days. Wonder about Lu Ann an think where is she? Little Man. Rod they put him away some place I dont know where. Cowboy dead. Most of them I guess back on the street. At first I miss it. But now I dont so much any more. I mean Man who need it? Man that one sue cio city an I dont care if I never see it again.

Right now I got the flower beds fixed for the winter. Cant hardly wait for the spring time to see how good I done.